Scottish Loch Summer Romance

De-ann Black

Paperback edition published 2024

Scottish Loch Summer Romance

ISBN: 9798880259489

Scottish Loch Summer Romance is the second book in the Scottish Loch Romance series.

1. Sewing & Mending Cottage
2. Scottish Loch Summer Romance
3. Sweet Music

The Sewing Bee
The Quilting Bee
Snow Bells Wedding
Snow Bells Christmas
Summer Sewing Bee
The Chocolatier's Cottage
Christmas Cake Chateau
The Beemaster's Cottage
The Sewing Bee By The Sea
The Flower Hunter's Cottage
The Christmas Knitting Bee
The Sewing Bee & Afternoon Tea
Shed In The City
The Bakery By The Seaside
The Christmas Chocolatier
The Christmas Tea Shop & Bakery
The Bitch-Proof Suit

Colouring books:
Summer Nature. Flower Nature. Summer Garden. Spring Garden. Autumn Garden. Sea Dream. Festive Christmas. Christmas Garden. Flower Bee. Wild Garden. Flower Hunter. Stargazer Space. Christmas Theme. Faerie Garden Spring. Scottish Garden Seasons. Bee Garden.

Embroidery books:
Floral Garden Embroidery Patterns
Floral Spring Embroidery Patterns
Christmas & Winter Embroidery Patterns
Floral Nature Embroidery Designs
Scottish Garden Embroidery Designs

Contents

Chapter One   1
Chapter Two   18
Chapter Three   32
Chapter Four   46
Chapter Five   60
Chapter Six   73
Chapter Seven   84
Chapter Eight   98
Chapter Nine   110
Chapter Ten   124
Chapter Eleven   138
Chapter Twelve   150

About De-ann Black   170

CHAPTER ONE

Robin's cottage glowed like a beacon in the night overlooking the beautiful loch in the Scottish Highlands. Lights shone from the windows, the front door was open in welcoming, and a wall lantern added a glow to the traditional whitewashed cottage.

The flowers in the garden had closed their petals after a full day in the sunlight, but a few evening fragrance flowers, like the night–scented stock, star jasmine, wisteria and night phlox perfumed the air, and their luminosity highlighted the cottage in hues of white, blue and lilac.

A dark, inky blue sky, scattered with stars, arched over the loch, the surrounding hills and nearby castle and estate. Spring had given way to summer, and the calm evening air was filled with the scent of greenery and flora and an undertone of excitement.

Several ladies from the local village's crafting bee chatted happily as they headed inside, carrying bags brimming with their sewing, quilting, knitting, embroidery and other items they were planning to work on.

Robin had organised an evening of crafting, tea and cake at her cottage. The weekly bee nights were held at the castle, owned by the laird, Gaven. The castle catered for hotel guests and functions. But Gaven had a wedding reception and a birthday celebration being held in the function room on the bee nights, so he'd had to cancel their crafting evenings for two weeks, promising to make it up to the members, which he always did when cancellations were required.

Not wishing to miss out, the ladies of the bee decided to hold their evenings at their own cottages. Robin had recently organised an evening at her cottage to show the members her techniques for creating her textile art. With the success of this, Robin was happy to hold a second night of chatter, cake and crafting.

Oliver had forgotten about this.

Armed with his artwork, a watercolour of her cottage that he'd painted for her, he stopped further along the loch and watched the ladies disappear inside, catching a glimpse of Robin welcoming them in. Her long, strawberry blonde hair fell in silky waves around her shoulders, and even at this distance, he admired her slender figure in her jeans and a pretty light blue top. She had porcelain skin, and was in her early thirties, marginally younger than Oliver. He was tall with a fit build, dark brown hair and green eyes, and wore classic casuals in muted tones.

He sighed heavily. He'd heard that Robin was holding a bee night, but in his excitement to impress her with the painting, he hadn't realised it was this evening.

He considered if he should go there anyway, give Robin the painting, and then leave. He'd planned to chat to her about art. Robin was a textile artist and a knitwear model. Her modelling earnings had helped support her as she established herself as a textile artist. But art was what they both had in common. Oliver's art shop, where he sold and displayed his watercolours, oils and acrylics of local landscapes and floral paintings, was in the main street. He lived above the shop and was a fairly recent newcomer to the village having moved in the previous summer.

His latest work was a collection of shop scenes depicting several of the local shops and their owners including — Bradoch and his bakery, the wee shop with the grocer, the tiny post office and postmaster, Fyn's flower shop, the pretty sweet shop with Sylvia's Aunt Muira, and Aileen's quilt shop. He'd been commissioned to paint the collection as artwork prints for a home decor company and had only just finished work on it. Robin's cottage wasn't part of the collection, but he'd painted it anyway in the hope that she'd like it.

Oliver had originally worked in the city, and found success as a popular artist. But he'd taken a holiday, an artist's break at one of the self–catering cabins at Gaven's castle the previous summer, and liked the village so much that he'd stayed to open his own shop. He planned to expand his collections while living in the beautiful Scottish Highlands, and so far his plan had worked.

Falling in love with Robin hadn't been part of his plans. She'd set up home in her cottage by the loch, and he'd found himself falling for her, even though he hardly knew her. He'd never been the overly confident type when it came to romance, and kept his feelings to himself.

But the local gossip, which was rife and usually fairly accurate, nailed him, that he was in love with one of the local ladies. Only recently, a few of the crafting bee ladies had surmised that it was Robin.

And he'd danced with her recently at the laird's party night at the castle. He'd plucked up the nerve to ask her to dance with him, and although she'd agreed and they'd waltzed around the floor, the evening had been drawing to a close and she'd been pulled back into the company of the crafting bee ladies at the end of the night. No more had happened since then. They'd both been extra busy with their work. But he had this niggling doubt that if he didn't make his feelings known to Robin, some other man would step into her life and he'd never get a chance to date her.

His plan had been to give her the painting and talk about art. He'd been impressed with a piece of fabric artwork she'd painted and hand stitched with embroidery thread. He'd seen it on her website. She'd painted an atmospheric sky on to white cotton fabric, and added pieces of colourful chiffon and lace to create a textured seascape. He'd been working on seascapes. This surely gave them something of interest to talk about. And then maybe...maybe he'd do what he'd been wanting to do for a while now — ask Robin to have dinner with him.

But he'd been scuppered. The timing was all wrong. He looked at the ladies heading into Robin's cottage and shook his head.

Standing beside the loch, it looked so still and calm, like dark glass reflecting the rolling hills around it, and the moon, a circle of white gold shining bright in the clear, starry sky. If ever there was a night for romance, the perfect setting...

He sighed wearily, and then headed back to his art shop in the main street, a two minute walk away.

There would be other nights, he consoled himself.

Etta helped Robin carry the tea and cake through to the living room and set it down on a table. Etta, a knitter and quilter with silvery blonde hair, lived on her own, and held regular craft nights at her cottage near the loch. In her fifties, with a neat appearance, she was a key member of the crafting bee and ran her small knitting business from her cottage.

Robin had bought a chocolate buttercream cake from Bradoch's bakery in the main street. Etta brought a home baked fruit cake, and other members contributed to the cake supply with fairy cakes.

Robin's work table was set up along with a sewing machine in her living room. The room was fairly large, with beige painted walls, a real log fire, unlit, and a wide window at the back looking out on to the lovely garden. She loved the kitchen too with its spacious and sturdy build with a kitchen table and chairs where she liked to sit, cosy and comfy, having her meals or sketching designs for her textile art. Her bedroom at the front of the cottage gave her a view of the loch at night. The perfect view to calm her senses after a busy day as she drifted off to sleep. In the past she'd thought a sea view would've been ideal, but a storm could cause the waves to wash on to the shore, and lash across the landscape, whereas even on wild days the loch looked calm.

The garden surrounded the cottage on all sides and the flowers provided colour and design ideas for her art. Her cottage was her home and studio.

Her art materials and desk were along one wall in the living room, and she had a chest of drawers where she kept a stash of fabric that she used for her textile art. A cream painted vintage dresser had shelves filled with paints and brushes, jars of beads and a wonderful selection of embroidery thread and crewel wool.

She'd organised folding chairs and a trestle table so that the members could work on their crafts. The members were keen to try their hand again at her textile art, and Robin was happy to do this. The bee nights were always fun.

Quilting and knitting were two very popular crafts that the bee members were skilled in, and most of them planned to work on these while welcoming any tips for textile art from Robin. Several of the members lived in cottages scattered around the hillside overlooking the loch, and with the village's main street only a couple of minutes walk away, this added to the close–knit friendship of the community.

'Help yourself to the tea and cake,' Robin told them as they took their jackets off and hung them on the back of their chairs. It was such a mild summer evening that many of them wore light clothing and cardigans they'd knitted themselves.

While the members helped themselves to tea and cake, the chatter included the latest gossip.

'Oh, this chocolate cake looks tasty,' said Aileen, owner of the local quilt shop. Aileen was around the same age as Robin, very attractive with a pale complexion, hazel eyes and dark brown hair. 'And the fruit cake looks equally tempting.'

'I bought the chocolate cake from Bradoch's bakery,' Robin explained. 'It's one of his new recipes. He's looking for feedback, so tuck in.'

Settling down to enjoy their tea and cake, the gossip began...

'Bradoch's got a thing for you,' Etta told Robin.

Robin almost choked on her cake. 'No he doesn't.'

'He does,' Aileen said, backing Etta.

'The local gossip likes to pair couples up,' Robin said, brushing aside their insistence.

'Bradoch's definitely got a wee fancy for you,' said Etta.

Robin was flattered, curious and thoughtful. But, romance wasn't something she was looking for this summer. With the spring tucked firmly behind them now, the warm weather had emerged, bringing with it the chance for her to work outdoors in the sunlight, in her garden, head to the nearby cove for a day at the shore. Go exploring the countryside. All these things were what she wanted to enjoy. Romance could complicate everything. Romance always did, at least in her experience. She wouldn't say she was unlucky in love, more like thwarted. Yes, that was an accurate description of the few and far between romantic encounters ranging from total disaster, mismatched, and what was I thinking dating him? Nope, getting involved, just when she wanted to be free to enjoy herself without any ties, commitments with a new boyfriend were not on her to–do list for the summer.

'Don't you think he's a handsome man?' Aileen said to Robin.

Robin's reply was casual. 'I suppose so, if you like that type.' She liked Bradoch. He was always cheery, and good looking, but not really her type. And she was sure he wasn't interested in her.

'Is Gaven, the laird, more your type?' Sylvia chipped–in. Sylvia, a green–eyed blonde with delicate features, and in her early thirties, worked at her aunt's sweet shop. They sold vintage, traditional and all sorts of sweets in the pretty little shop.

'No,' said Robin. 'Gaven's obviously handsome, but I just don't feel that frisson, you know what I mean.'

They did.

'What about Fyn at the flower shop? Does he ring your bell?' Etta said with a cheeky grin.

'Etta!' Robin scolded her with a smile.

'Well, he's a handsome one,' said Etta. 'All blond hair, light blue eyes and chiselled features.'

'Fyn fancies Aileen,' Sylvia remarked.

Aileen nearly dropped her cake in her tea. 'He does not!'

'He does so,' Sylvia insisted.

Aileen was deeply flattered. She liked Fyn, though she hadn't noticed him paying her any special attention.

'We're lucky,' said Sylvia. 'It's one of those times when there are a few good looking and eligible men living in the community.' She looked thoughtful. 'They'll probably all be snapped up by Christmas.'

'It's only the start of the summer,' Robin reminded her.

'I know, but time flies, especially when it comes to romance,' said Sylvia.

Etta held up a jumper she was knitting. 'This is a pattern for a winter jumper. The summer is the time when I start making all my gifts and crafts for Christmas.'

Aileen agreed. 'I've made a start on a snowman quilt that I won't sell in my shop until Christmas.'

'Have you got snowman fabric?' Etta said, sounding interested.

'Yes, it's through the back of my shop in my storeroom,' Aileen explained. 'I don't want to put it on sale in the summer, out of season.'

'You should,' Etta insisted. 'This is when we buy a lot of our Christmas fabric. Quilts take a while to make, at least, mine do.'

Other members encouraged Aileen to sell the Christmas fabric.

'I'll display a wee range of the festive fabric in the front shop,' Aileen agreed.

'Great,' said Etta. 'I'll pop in during the morning and have a browse.'

The chatter and crafting continued, and Robin showed them a piece of her textile art.

'This is what I'm working on at the moment. It's the background for another seascape. I've added a watercolour wash to the cotton. I'm planning to pop to the cove and sketch the coast to help me create the design of the artwork.' Robin let them see her work. The last time they'd been to her cottage, she demonstrated her method of painting watercolour on to the cotton fabric to create a background for her designs, and sewing on pieces of fabric to make a seascape. 'And this is another new design. I'm making a summer floral piece, a cottage garden, using fabric scraps, watercolour, ribbon trims, pieces of lace and beads to give the impression of cornflowers, roses, and all sorts of bright coloured flowers.'

'I love how you've layered the flowers,' Etta enthused. 'It looks like a summer garden.'

'I'm going to add a cottage,' said Robin, eyeing her work.

'A cottage would look gorgeous,' Etta agreed.

'Speaking of gorgeous...' Sylvia motioned out the window. 'There's Gaven going for his run along the loch.'

Gaven was tall and fit, in his mid–thirties, with rich auburn hair and grey–green eyes.

'He's a fine looking man,' said Etta.

'You should see the new guest that's booked in to one of the castle's cabins,' Jessy announced. In her fifties, she wore her brown hair pinned up in a tidy bun. Jessy worked at the castle, and as a member of the bee, she updated the ladies on everything that went on there. 'He's an artist, in his mid–thirties, and very elegant and handsome. He's on holiday for two weeks.'

The castle was a hotel, catering for guests throughout the year. Gaven had specially–built cabins on the castle's estate offering self–catering accommodation for guests wishing to relax and work on their crafts. Writers, artists and designers had been the main guests at the cabins. Movie stars had also been guests at the castle and cabins, but mainly it catered for authors and artists with the cabins kitted out with writing desks, comfy sofas, art easels and windows that let in plenty of light.

'He sounds lovely,' said Sylvia.

As they discussed the new guest, they noticed Gaven running back along the loch.

'Gaven's looking up here,' said Sylvia, giving him a wave.

'No, he'll think we're watching him,' Etta hissed at her.

'He's pretending not to notice,' said Sylvia. 'Now he's running back to the castle.'

'Have any of you ever had a look at his turret?' Robin said to them.

'No, none of us have ever been invited,' said Aileen. 'Though Penny came close to getting an invitation up to his private turret.'

'Where is Penny?' one of the ladies asked, glancing around the company. Penny was an expert at sewing and mending techniques and a newcomer to the community.

'Penny's away for a couple of weeks to Edinburgh on business and pleasure,' Etta explained. 'As her cottage is near mine, I'm keeping an eye on it while she's gone.'

'I've had a peek inside the castle turret,' Jessy told them. 'Gaven's got a view of the loch.'

Sylvia sighed. 'How romantic.'

'Ah, so you've got a fancy for our laird,' Jessy surmised.

'Most women think he's handsome, and the castle is an enticement too. Imagine living in a castle and spending romantic nights with the laird in his turret,' said Sylvia.

A moment's lull settled over the ladies as many of them considered this scenario.

'But chance would be a fine thing,' Sylvia said to them. 'Gaven's not interested in me.'

Gaven kept up a steady pace as he powered up the hill towards the castle. He ran along the loch most nights. It helped him unwind after a hectic day tending to the guests and overseeing the running of the castle and the estate. He was fine with the responsibility he'd inherited and wouldn't change it, but there were times when he longed to have someone to share it with. A short string of past romances made him wonder if he'd ever find the woman for him. For now, he ran away any tension of the day and frustrations.

He ran through the castle's main entrance and headed towards the front door. A dinner dance was being held in the function room, and he hurried by and up the stairs to his turret bedroom to shower and change. Often he'd run very late at night when the dinners and parties were finished and guests had retired for the evening. But he'd decided to run in the early evening, and hopefully have an early night. He was up at the crack of dawn in the morning to welcome another guest to one of the self–catering cabins. A good night's sleep was what he needed.

Striping off his running gear, he jumped in the shower and then got ready for bed.

The lights of the village flickered in the distance, and the loch glowed in the moonlight. A picture perfect scene. Something the new guest, an artist, a man around the same age as himself, with a reasonable amount of success, could be interested in painting. Apparently, he'd been commissioned to paint several pieces for limited edition prints as part of his new collection.

Gaven was about to go to bed when there was a knock on his door.

He opened it to find Walter, a sturdy man in his fifties, and a member of the castle's staff, standing there.

'Sorry to disturb you, Gaven, but that new artist, the one that booked into a cabin, would like a word with you. He's downstairs in the function room bar.'

Gaven nodded and started to throw on a shirt, tie and smart pair of dark trousers. 'Did he say what he wants to talk to me about?'

'Something to do with wanting one of the locals to give him a tour of the area, especially the cove. Someone with artistic leanings.'

Gaven put on his tie and swept his still damp auburn hair back from his handsome face. He frowned at Walter.

Walter shrugged.

'Oliver would be my first suggestion,' said Gaven, and then hurried from the turret, down the winding staircase, along to the elegant reception and into the function room.

Walter disappeared back into the melee of guests while Gaven approached the artist sitting at a table in the bar area.

'I understand you wanted to talk to me,' Gaven began.

'Yes,' said Jonathan, elegant in both attire and manner. 'I'd like you to ask someone local, preferably an artist, to show me around the area. It would save me trudging over the hills, around the loch and the farmland to find ideal locations for my artwork. And to look for the cove that's apparently a hidden niche. I'm here to paint landscapes and seascapes, not to tour the area. Do you know of anyone suitable?'

'Oliver. He's a wonderfully talented artist. He owns his own art shop in the main street.'

Jonathan's shrewd eyes looked like a storm had suddenly started brewing in them, and he pushed an elegant hand through his silky, light brown hair that had a tendency to flop over his forehead. 'No, no...he's probably tied to his shop and not able to freely show me around.'

Gaven nodded. 'Yes, that's true. He has his shop to attend.' Then he had another suggestion. 'But we do have a local textile artist. Robin works from home in her cottage near the loch.'

Jonathan's reluctant expression lifted. 'What's she like?'

'Very talented, very pleasant. A lovely young woman,' Gaven summarised. And then he checked her website on his phone. He held up a picture of Robin and her bio.

Jonathan's expression lifted further. 'A textile artist. I see she mentions seascapes and landscapes. Could you call her and ask if she'd help me out?'

'Yes.' Gaven went to call, and then he had an idea. 'The ladies of the crafting bee are at Robin's cottage this evening. One of my key staff, Jessy, is there. I'll call her and ask her to have a word with Robin.'

'Perfect,' Jonathan agreed.

The ladies were chatting about quilting when Jessy's phone rang. 'It's Gaven,' she told them, frowning. 'I wonder if there's something wrong.'

Everyone stopped stitching, knitting and embroidering as Jessy took the call.

'Jessy,' Gaven began. 'Could you ask Robin if she's available tomorrow to show one of our new guests, Jonathan the artist, around the area.' He explained the details.

Jessy brightened. 'Yes, Robin's right here. I'll ask her.' She told Robin what he wanted.

'Show the guest around the area? The cove?' Robin wanted to clarify.

'Yes.' Jessy sounded enthusiastic. 'Are you busy tomorrow morning?'

'Eh, no, not especially. I was planning to go to the cove anyway so—'

'Robin says she's happy to help him,' Jessy told Gaven, causing Robin to blink. She'd barely thought this through. 'After breakfast? Ah, have breakfast at the castle? Yes, lovely. Okay. Bye.'

Etta and the other ladies exchanged an excited glance.

'Gaven has invited you to have breakfast at the castle with Jonathan. You'll like Jonathan,' Jessy told

Robin. 'He's very suave. Very artistic. And very handsome.'

Robin wasn't sure if she was happy or perturbed.

'Gaven is grateful to you for helping him out,' Jessy assured Robin. 'He says he's going to make it up to you. And Gaven always keeps his word when it comes to things like that.'

'Gaven doesn't need to,' said Robin. 'I'm heading to the cove anyway. Maybe chatting about seascapes with another artist will be fun.'

'Gaven was going to ask Oliver,' Jessy explained. 'But then he realised he's tied to his shop.'

This seemed reasonable to Robin and the others.

Robin then put the kettle on to make another round of tea. The chatter and gossip continued.

'Has Oliver made any move on you recently?' Sylvia said to Robin. 'We all thought he was in love with one of the local ladies. We assumed it was you. And he did ask you to dance with him at the castle party.'

'I danced with Gaven, Fyn, Bradoch, some of the farmers, and Oliver,' Robin explained.

Etta was curious. 'So Oliver hasn't asked you out or anything like that since you were dancing?'

Robin shook her head. 'No. I told you he wasn't interested in me. You know what the local gossip is like.'

Etta nodded thoughtfully. 'I guess we were wrong about Oliver.'

The other members agreed.

Pushing all thoughts of Oliver aside, they enjoyed another round of tea and cake and continued with their evening of crafting — and chatting about Jonathan the suave and sexy artist.

CHAPTER TWO

By the glow of the display lights in his shop, Oliver tucked the watercolour of Robin's cottage safely into an art portfolio. Her cottage had looked lovely tonight in the evening light beside the loch, and so too did Robin.

He sighed deeply and gazed out the front window at the main street, lit with streetlamps and twinkle lights stretching the full length of it. It was worthy of a painting. Traditionally picturesque.

Deciding that he would paint it, he stepped outside and snapped photos of the quaint shops lining the street. He'd painted several of the shops as individual pieces, watercolours with an illustrative effect, but he hadn't painted them as a whole, a scene that he imagined would benefit from the night–time's glow.

Checking he had the photos he needed, he breathed in the mild night air, glanced at the floral watercolour paintings on display in the window, went back inside his shop and locked the door against a night that made him feel like he'd missed a chance to talk to Robin.

But there was always tomorrow night, he told himself, wandering through to the shop's kitchen to make a cup of tea, knowing he wouldn't settle if he went to bed, and eager to view the pictures on his laptop.

The kitchen's vintage decor included the original blue and white tiles on the walls near the two butler sinks. Many of the shops in the main street were converted from the authentic buildings of years gone by. Living at the back or above the shops was popular, as was retaining the original decor. Oliver used one sink for cleaning his brushes, water jars and washing the paint off his hands — the mucky but colourful sink with splashes of paint over it. The second sink was used for making tea and cooking, even though he had a small kitchen upstairs, this was the one he used most with its old–fashioned looking cooker. Anything new that he'd added, he bought with vintage or classic styling and design. The tall wooden dresser stored a mismatched range of dinner plates, mugs and ceramic teapots. Jars of watercolour brushes sat amid the crockery on the shelves, and he'd hand–painted the entire dresser eau–de–nil. Wooden stools were painted robin egg blue.

Sipping a cup of tea, he poured through the images of the main street, and settled on one that captured the feeling he was looking for — a traditional village main street with pretty shops set against an inky sky full of stars.

Itching to see if he could sketch that feeling on to paper, he opened up a large, artwork pad of smooth, white paper, picked up a fine tip mechanical pencil, and began drawing a rough outline of what he had in mind.

As the concept started to take shape, he erased any extraneous lines, and kept sketching until he had a finished pencil drawing of the scene.

Holding it at arm's length, he studied it with a critical eye, and then smiled to himself. If he could paint this scene, add the rich colours, the vast dark blue sky scattered with stars, the shops with their windows filled with everything from flowers and fashion to sweets and cakes, it could make an impressive addition to his artwork collection of shops.

Resisting the temptation to set up his watercolours to paint it, he put the sketch pad away, turned the lights off and went upstairs to bed with the intention of getting a good night's sleep.

Lying in bed, his night–time view was always of the sky from his bedroom window. The converted cottage had a cosy living room, bedroom, kitchen and bathroom upstairs. He'd painted the living room walls pale cream. The polished wooden floor had a large cream rug that added to the light atmosphere. The sofa and chairs were an eclectic mix of creams and florals, positioned for comfort in front of the fire. His paintings created splashes of colour to the light decor, with oil landscapes and seascapes and large floral watercolours.

Off the living room, the little kitchen provided a snug space overlooking the back garden where he enjoyed pottering around. Part tidy where the lawn was cut, and part wild where the climbing roses and other rambling florals looked like they were making a run for it over the hedging that bordered the garden. A small shed was tucked at the side and had an old–fashioned horse shoe nailed above the door, the right way up so that apparently the luck didn't fall out.

This summer he planned to devote more time to his garden, tending to it and relaxing on lovely sunny days and mellow evenings.

Gazing out the bedroom window at the stars, he thought about Robin. Maybe he'd pop along to her cottage in the morning, before he opened up his shop for the day, and give her the painting. Bradoch's bakery opened early, so he aimed to buy fresh rolls and tattie scones and take them along for her breakfast.

Robin lay tucked up in bed gazing out at the loch that looked so calm and unruffled, unlike her.

Breakfast at the castle should be fun, she bolstered herself. Meeting a successful artist and showing him around the area, including a trip to the cove, would be nice. She'd checked him out online. Pictures showed a handsome, tall, elegant man with a penchant for wearing attire that wouldn't be out of place in a vintage drama. Cream linen shirts, sometimes worn open neck with a classic jumper, or with a silk cravat tied just right. She'd studied his face, clean–shaven, again with a look that could put him on the set of a vintage drama without fussing too much. Well–cut, light brown hair was short at the back and sides with a full floppy length on top that emphasised his eyes when he peered out from under it. She couldn't fathom the colour of his eyes, and as she had an artist's eye for distinguishing specific hues, this was unusual. Rather like Jonathan, she thought, settling on the feeling of a colour that described his eyes as close as she could manage — shrewd dark grey, steely, watchful. The overall impression from Jonathan was that he never missed a trick.

Refusing to let any sinking thoughts weigh her down, she gazed out at her favourite view of the loch and went to sleep.

The morning was bright, one of those light, early summer days filled with potential.

Oliver was up extra sharp and bounded over to Bradoch's bakery, a two–storey bakery in the heart of the main street. He wasn't the first customer. Etta had popped in for her morning rolls and scones and he saw her walking away down the road.

The scent of fresh baked bread and cakes ignited Oliver's appetite as he headed into the bakery. He wore dark cords and a light blue shirt, casual but clean and smart. His hair was still slightly damp from showering and was swept back from his handsome face.

'Morning, Oliver.' Bradoch went to bag the usual order for him. 'You're up with the lark today.'

'Yes, a busy day planned.' Oliver sounded chirpy.

Bradoch was around the same age and height as Oliver, early thirties and a tall, fine looking man with dark hair and dark blue eyes. Trained as a patisserie chef, he'd taken over the bakery from his grandfather. He wore chef's whites and a welcoming smile.

The bakery had a modern vintage vibe. Spotlights highlighted the glass counter and display cabinets brimming with cakes, scones, pastries and various patisserie specials including the popular glazed fruit tarts and chocolate cake.

The fire in the hearth at the front of the bakery, where a few tables enabled customers to enjoy a cake and a cuppa, was unlit in anticipation that the day would bring its own warmth.

Bradoch sensed Oliver was up to something special and paused from bagging the usual order of two rolls and a sliced pan loaf. 'What can I get for you?'

'Four rolls, six tattie scones and...' he paused and viewed the cakes.

'Fancy something special this morning?'

'Eh, yes...do you happen to know what type of cakes Robin likes.'

'Robin?'

Oliver nodded and smiled tightly.

'She likes anything with cream. A classic Victoria sponge, a scone filled with strawberry jam and whipped cream, a wee fruit trifle.' Bradoch paused. 'Why? Are you thinking of buying her a treat?'

With no one within earshot, Oliver confided in Bradoch. 'I've done a watercolour painting of her cottage, as a gift. I thought I'd take it to her this morning, along with something tasty for her breakfast.'

Bradoch frowned and bit his lip.

'What? Is there something wrong?'

'I hate to burst your bubble, Oliver, but Etta was just in. She told me that Gaven has invited Robin to have breakfast at the castle. He's asked her to show one of the new guests, an artist called Jonathan, around the area, the loch, a trip to the seaside cove, to give him inspiration for his new collection of landscape and seascape paintings.'

Oliver blinked. The information overload hit him hard, knocking his intentions in all directions like scattered marbles.

Bradoch could see the shock on Oliver's face. 'I'm awfy sorry.'

'An artist?' Oliver sounded lost.

'He's apparently fairly successful, though we've never heard of him, and I'm sure he's not a patch on you. But he's staying at one of the self–catering cabins at the castle. Isn't that what you did? You came to the castle for a wee break last summer and ended up moving here.'

'I did.' Now he had the horrible thought that this Jonathan person would do the same. 'What's he like? Do you know anything about him?'

'Etta said the ladies were all a flutter talking about him last night at Robin's cottage. Jessy told them he's sexy and suave, and he's around the same age as you and me.'

'So, he's handsome.'

'That doesn't mean that Robin will fancy him.' Bradoch heard himself sound less convincing than he'd intended.

Oliver's mind was whirring, trying to make sense of the information. 'Why did the laird ask Robin to be Jonathan's tour guide?'

'You were Gaven's first choice, but then Jonathan said that if you had a shop you probably wouldn't have the time to show him around. That's when Gaven suggested Robin.' He told him the details that Etta had mentioned.

Oliver's heart sank. 'Thanks for telling me. I'll take my usual order.'

'Can I tempt you with a savoury cheesy pastry? You could heat it up for your lunch. And maybe a snowball.' Bradoch motioned to the snowball cakes covered in white icing.

Oliver nodded, clearly deflated. 'Yes, pop them in as well.' He paid for the items and then trudged back to his art shop, hopes dashed.

Robin drove to the castle, not knowing if Jonathan had transport or would require her to drive him around the area. Besides, she had her travel watercolour kit with her, a compact set of paints and brushes that was ideal for painting outdoors. A sketch pad, watercolour pad, a bottle of water, pencils and other bits and pieces were tucked into her sturdy bag that had pockets and dookits for holding everything she needed for outdoor artwork. And a blanket. Plus two folding chairs in the boot of the car. Usually she perched on a wall or hillside, with or without using a blanket, to paint outdoors, but with Jonathan in tow, and having folding chairs from the bee night, she thought these could be handy. Snacks wouldn't be necessary. They were always going to be within munching distance of the bakery in the main street, her cottage, the castle, or the cove where she'd yet to sample the delights of the local seaside bakery restaurant renowned for its delicious, top class lunches and ice cream.

She wore slim–fitting grey cords, comfy black pumps, a short sleeve white blouse and a light grey cardigan. Her long hair fell in silky waves around her shoulders. Makeup was minimal, with neutral tone eye shadow and black mascara emphasising her blue eyes.

The drive to the castle was so short she hadn't even finished sorting out her thoughts and plans by the time she drove up and parked near the front entrance.

She blinked against the bright sunlight shining through a cloudless blue sky above the impressive structure of the castle. It was something she should design as a piece of textile art, she thought to herself, wondering what textures of fabric and embroidery thread she'd use to create the castle and impressive turrets. Which one was Gaven's turret? Probably the one on the right. It would have a view of the loch. Different from her view, his would look down on it and the surrounding countryside. She pictured it would look magical at night, though she preferred the view she had right on her doorstep and firmly grounded.

Jonathan was staying in one of the luxury self–catering cabins within the estate where the trees created a forest–like setting. From the information she'd seen online, he'd reached a reasonably high level of success, and his new art collections were keenly anticipated. He painted landscapes and seascapes, mainly oils and acrylics though a few watercolours depending on the collection. Limited edition prints of his work sold well, as did the originals.

Walking into the traditional and stylish reception, she realised she hadn't been inside the castle during the day — only in the evenings when attending the crafting bee nights or for dances and party functions.

In the evenings, it was aglow with sparkle from the chandeliers and other lights. But here, in the morning, with the front entrance wide open letting in the fresh air, it looked bright with sunlight streaming through the windows of the function room and other rooms including one where she would be having breakfast.

'Ah, Robin,' Gaven's voice wafted over to her as he bounded, well–dressed in his suit, down the main staircase to welcome her. 'Thank you for coming at such short notice. Jonathan's already been hard at work painting in his cabin since first light.' He gestured towards a room at the front of the castle. 'We're through here for breakfast.'

Robin smiled and got ready to meet her companion for the day.

'It's a lovely, bright morning,' Gaven said to her as he led her over to a table near the window where the sunlight streamed in without dazzling them.

'Yes,' Robin agreed. 'It's beautiful, and warm already. I think we're in for a scorcher.'

Jonathan's eyes took in the beautiful young woman walking over to where he was seated at the table for breakfast. He'd ordered, but hadn't yet been served with his poached eggs on wholemeal toast, with smoked salmon and garnished with watercress and cherry tomatoes.

He was pleased to see that Robin's photograph on her website bio hadn't falsely flattered her. Meeting her for real, he considered her to be even lovelier. The day with her was certainly going to be a scorcher even if it poured with rain, which was likely as the Scottish weather was somewhat fickle. Hopefully, Robin was not. Her smile as she approached him made her look pleasant and friendly. She appeared to be genuine, so he smiled in kind and extended his hand.

'I'm delighted to meet you, Robin. And thank you for agreeing to show me around the area.'

Jonathan's well–spoken voice sounded cut–glass clear, and his hand felt smooth and elegant with long fingers and manicured nails free from any evidence that he was an artist. Usually there was a hint of paint, a fleck of acrylic, a tint from the watercolours, inky fingers from drawing. But Jonathan's hands were perfectly clean. Nothing. Not even a smudge.

If Gaven hadn't mentioned that Jonathan had been up early painting, she wouldn't have been suspicious. But she shrugged off her doubts, and sat down to order breakfast.

'I'll have a soufflé omelette,' she told the waiter, handing back the menu. 'And a pot of breakfast tea.'

'Well,' said Gaven. 'I'll let you two become acquainted and get on with your day.' He left to get on with his.

'I had a look at your textile art on your website,' Jonathan told her. 'I've never dabbled in textiles, but I can appreciate your work, especially the landscapes.'

'I'm planning to create new seascapes and intended heading to the cove. It's not far, and it's a lovely sunny day to enjoy a visit to the shore.'

'Perfect. We'll have breakfast and then we'll set off for a day of artistic adventure.'

Jonathan smiled at her, and she smiled back, feeling hopeful that their day would be fun.

'I drove here. Do you have a car, or shall we use mine?' she said.

'My car is at the cabin, but let's go in yours. You know your way around the area. It'll be easier.'

She agreed this made sense. 'I packed a couple of folding chairs in case we need them.'

Jonathan looked impressed. 'That was very thoughtful of you, Robin.'

Hearing him say her name, so eloquent and with a smile on his handsome face, affected her senses. She wasn't attracted to Jonathan she told herself firmly. Okay, so he was exactly as Jessy had described. Suave and sexy. But totally not her type.

As they finished breakfast and headed out to her car, chatting happily about their favourite paints and brushes, she began to wonder if perhaps she might like Jonathan a little bit more than she'd first thought.

Robin drove them away from the castle, opening the windows to let the warm air waft in.

'Is that the local loch?' Jonathan pointed over to it.

'Yes, and that's my cottage over there, slightly up on the hillside overlooking it.'

'What a beautiful cottage. I assume you work from home.'

'I do. My desk and artwork is set up in the living room. I love what I do, so I don't mind combining both. It's a pretty cottage and more spacious than it looks. And the garden is wonderful.'

'Plenty of inspiration for your textile art florals.'

She glanced at him. 'You really have poured over my website, haven't you?'

'Of course. I wanted to find out about this talented and lovely textile artist the laird was recommending to show me around the area.'

Robin laughed.

'The laird's words, not mine, though having met you and seen your work, I'm inclined to agree with him.'

Robin felt a blush form across her cheeks at his flattery and was glad the windows were open to feel the breeze.

'Where's the village's main street from here?' Jonathan wanted to know, trying to figure out the lay of the land.

'We're about to drive along it. It's only a couple of minutes from the loch. The community is quite close–knit.'

Robin followed the road from the loch on to the main street.

'It's so picturesque,' he remarked, admiring the shops as they drove past. Then he noticed the paintings on display in the art shop window. 'Is that Oliver's art shop?'

'Yes, do you want to pop in and see him before we drive to the coast?' she offered.

'No, no,' he said firmly. 'Let's make the most of the morning.'

Robin smiled and drove them on to the road leading to the coast.

Jonathan surreptitiously glanced back at Oliver's large watercolour floral paintings, admitting to himself that they were impressive, but keeping his thoughts to himself.

'Is there somewhere we can have lunch at the coast, or will we need to head back for that?'

'There's a bakery restaurant that I'm told serves wonderful lunches.'

'We'll explore the coast for suitable subject matter for painting, and then pop there for lunch. My treat.'

Robin felt herself looking forward to the entire trip with Jonathan. 'With ice cream?' she added, smiling at him.

'No trip to the seaside is complete without ice cream. What's your favourite flavour. No, let me guess...strawberry.'

Robin glanced at him. 'How did you know?'

'You look like a strawberry ice cream type of young lady to me.'

She eyed him and guessed what his favourite flavour was. 'Chocolate or classic vanilla.'

'The classic is certainly my taste. But strawberry comes a close second.'

'I might share mine with you, if you're on your best behaviour,' she joked with him.

He sighed, playing along. 'No strawberry for me then. I'm bad when it comes to good behaviour.'

Something in his sexy smile warned her this was true. But enjoying herself in his company, she tucked the warning away and drove on into the sunshine as the scent of the sea began to waft in the windows, along with a sense of adventure.

CHAPTER THREE

Oliver threw himself into his work. But even though he hurled himself into painting the starry sky scene of the main street shops, he couldn't stop thinking about Robin — and how he'd missed his chance to talk to her last night and this morning.

He mixed Prussian blue with water to create the first wash of the night sky, fading it down to the shop rooftops. The wash shimmered under the light on his artwork desk and he added a hint of deep blue to the top of the fade, capturing the depth of colours from the photographs he'd taken.

Other layers were painted across the large sheet of cold pressed watercolour paper that was thick enough to withstand the technique without warping. The edges were taped down to hold it steady while he worked on the night sky.

Then he started with light grey and sepia washes on the rooftops of the shops, and made the windows come to life with warm yellow. When these were dry, he used a long, thin, rigger brush to sweep inky blue and dark grey lines along the edges of the buildings, windows and doors, emphasising them like an illustration.

He used a round brush and grey tones to create a couple of figures walking past the shops. He liked to include people in his paintings, even if they were only a shadowy hint of a couple meandering along highlighted by the warm yellow glow.

But all the while his mind was picturing Robin and Jonathan having fun at the cove. He'd seen them driving by in her small red car, taking the coast road heading to the sea. He'd hoped one summer's day to take Robin there for lunch at the bakery restaurant. To go swimming and enjoy the sunshine and white sand bay.

He sighed wearily. By dragging his heels he'd lost out to Jonathan.

Then something in him stirred. A flicker of hope. That spark of determination that so often helped him forge ahead, and make substantial success for himself as an artist. No mean feat.

Come on, he urged himself. The sun's shining. It was approaching lunchtime. Close the shop for the rest of the day and head to the coast. Faint heart and all that...

Throwing his swimming trunks on, that were like aqua boxer shorts, then putting his cords back on, he stuffed a towel in a duffel bag, secured the shop, and put a notice in the window for customers to contact him via his website. He doubted he'd miss out on business as everyone was probably taking advantage of the sunshine, outside in their gardens, at the loch, the castle's estate or the cove. People were meandering along the main street eating ice lollies from the wee shop.

Oliver cast the duffel bag in the back seat of his car and headed in search of a second chance, or was it a third chance, with Robin. He wasn't counting. The only thing he was counting on was that she was at the cove with Jonathan. If not, he'd go for a swim anyway.

Sunny days like this were made for having fun, not for moping in the shadows.

He opened the car windows, breathing in the warm air. The sun was at its height and the cloudless cerulean sky gave no hint that it intended cooling down any time soon. It was one of those days, he thought, that you remember when you look back, that's filled with warmth and sunshine.

Jonathan untied his cravat, but kept it around his open neck shirt. Other than that, his waistcoat remained buttoned up, as did Jonathan. Sitting on one of the folding chairs on the white sand, nestled near the dunes, fringed with long grass and sea thistles, he borrowed Robin's sketch pad and pencils to draw a rough outline of the cove view in front of him.

Robin sat on a dune behind him. The navy blue silk on the back of his dark waistcoat shone like watered ink in the bright sunlight.

She took photos of the cove and the sparkling sea with her phone. She hadn't brought a spare sketchpad, and as Jonathan seemed eager to capture the essence of the view, as he described it, he'd asked to use hers. He'd apologised for not thinking ahead and bringing his own, but...

The cove was reasonably busy. People were in swimming, paddling, playing on the sand, and the bakery restaurant and other brightly painted, tiny shops in the heart of the cove were buzzing with customers.

'We should start thinking about lunch soon,' Robin said to him.

He raised a hand, as if not wanting to be disturbed from his artistic bubble at that precise moment.

She sort of understood, and didn't push it. She still felt well–fed on the castle's breakfast, though a cup of tea wouldn't have gone amiss. Scolding herself for not bringing a flask of tea, she focussed on the view of the sea, squinting against the dazzling sunbeams reflecting off the surface.

The water was turquoise. Turquoise! And the white sand was a triumph of nature, as was the cove itself. The bay wrapped itself around a length of the coast, and there was no hint that the countryside, rolling hills and the loch were nearby.

She sighed happily and felt the warmth of the sun, feeling fortunate to have such a beautiful seashore close to home.

Far in the distance, small boats with colourful sails navigated the coast, and beyond those was the hazy outline of Scottish islands.

She'd suggested to Jonathan that they go for a walk along the north part of the cove where the view of the islands would make a perfect backdrop to any painting, but he dismissed this idea and took them in the opposite direction until they were in the thick of the dunes where the terrain was rougher. She thought the view was far less interesting, though still lovely with the sea lapping on to the coast in front of them.

While walking around taking pictures, she'd peeked at his sketches, and it seemed that he was drawing no more than roughs without any details or anchoring aspects. He could've drawn that anywhere, but she shrugged off her doubts and left him to it.

Breathing in the fresh sea air, and loving the warmth of the sun, she planned what she'd use to create her own textile art — gorgeous pieces of turquoise chiffon depicting the sea, with layers of aquamarine tulle and silk. She could imagine hand stitching it with embroidery thread in tones of blues and greens, and adding strips of lace she'd dyed in shades of blue. The sky, as she gazed up, shielding her eyes from the intensity was a fantastic cobalt blue. Perhaps she'd be equally bold and make the skyline one dynamic band of cobalt, something a bit different for her new seascape collection.

A few sea birds seemed to effortlessly glide across the sky, and she photographed two cormorants in mid-flight. She always liked to add birds, butterflies, bees and other creatures to her work.

Bumblebees were enjoying buzzing around the wildflowers on the dunes, and she took pictures of those too, imagining she'd make a feature of one of the bumbles with crewel wool to give it a fuzzy texture and then add gossamer chiffon wings and embroider it with cotton and gold metallic thread.

She glanced at Jonathan, still sketching away, so she left him to it and got on with her own design ideas.

Oliver pulled up in the car park. It was fairly busy, as he'd expected. He looked around and there was Robin's red car. His heart soared. She was still here. Now all he had to do was find her amid the revellers.

The air was a tonic, and he took a moment to breathe it in. The aroma of tasty lunches wafted from the bakery restaurant, and a couple of mobile food vans and stalls selling savoury snacks. He might be tempted to treat himself to a chip piece with tomato sauce and fried onions.

He'd skipped breakfast because he was too perturbed. He hadn't even had a sniff of his snowball. But he was fired up on the hope of finding Robin, though he'd no idea what he'd say to her, or any plan of action. He aimed to wing it rather than miss the boat yet again.

Stripping down to his trunks and a pair of canvas shoes, he stashed his phone in the glove compartment, locked the car and walked across to where the restaurant was and then down on to the lovely white sand.

Standing in the midst of the activity around him, he cupped his hand to shield his eyes from the dazzling sunlight and shimmer off the sea, searching for Robin. He expected she'd be with a suave and sexy man, so he was on the lookout for the two of them. But there was no sign of them, not even from the numerous heads bobbing in the sea from those in swimming. And there were quite a few swimmers in the sparkling turquoise sea. It looked so tempting that Oliver decided to give in to temptation.

Kicking off his shoes, he walked into the water and began swimming along the coast, every now and then, diving below the surface, gazing around at the clear, turquoise water. It felt like swimming in the vivid cerulean watercolour he used to paint seas and skies. The water was so clear he could see the ripples on the sand and white pebbles dotted around.

Bobbing to the surface, he treaded water and looked along the shore, still searching for any sign of Robin. Nothing. No sign of her anywhere.

He swam on, enjoying the first swim of the summer. He hadn't been swimming since last summer, and intended making the most of the cove in the coming months. Yes, there would be days of rain and grey skies, but this area of Scotland benefited from being shielded by the outlying islands.

Emerging again from underwater, he blinked against the sunlight — and his heart soared when he saw Robin, sitting in the dunes. Presumably the man sitting nearby was Jonathan. Was that a waistcoat he was wearing?

Telling himself to buck up, he swam to the shore.

Robin had no idea he was heading her way until...

The tall, lean and fit figure of Oliver, striding out of the sea, dripping wet, pushing his hair back from his handsome face, waved to her.

'Oliver!' she exclaimed, totally surprised. For a moment she wondered if it was him. She hadn't seen him with his clothes off. Or rather, wearing swimming trunks. Her heart reacted instantly to his strong, lean build. The long muscles in his thighs gave him an athletic look. She knew Oliver was tall and trim, but hadn't anticipated quite how...virile he looked striding out of the water and walking towards her.

Jonathan saw Robin's reaction first, and then glared at Oliver, resenting having his day interrupted, especially by somewhat of an artistic rival. He'd checked out the competition as well as reading Robin's website, and saw what a talented artist this

Oliver person actually was. His shop's website showed an impressive range of paintings. Not that he intended telling Oliver this. They were potential rivals, and maybe not just when it came to their art. He saw the way Oliver gazed at Robin, clearly smitten with her, but without the confidence to do anything about it. That was fine. But Robin's reaction when she saw Oliver bothered him. He disliked sharing the limelight with anyone, especially another artist like Oliver. And he sensed a spark of interest in Oliver from Robin.

'What are you doing here?' Robin said to Oliver as he now stood in front of her with droplets of sea water trickling down his lean torso. His trunks clung to his thighs and other parts that she tried and failed not to glance at. She hadn't realised how athletic looking Oliver was.

'Enjoying the sunshine,' said Oliver. It wasn't a lie, just not quite the truth.

'I didn't recognise you at first without your clothes on,' Robin told him. 'No, what I mean is, with nothing on except your trunks.' That sounded only marginally better and she blushed at her own awkward comments.

Oliver smiled. 'Are you having fun?' The green of his eyes bore an extra intensity when he glanced at Jonathan.

'Sorry, this is Jonathan,' she said, hurriedly introducing them. 'He's taking an artist's retreat break at one of the cabins at the castle.'

Neither men made any move to step forward to shake hands, and only a curt nod of acknowledgement passed between them. This was the first time they'd met, and yet they both knew who the other was. Oliver had never been envious of another artist's ability, but he felt a stab of jealousy seeing Jonathan with Robin.

'Are you going in for a swim?' Oliver said to them. 'The sea's mild and the water's so clear.'

Robin hesitated, realising she hadn't even thought about going for a swim. Her focus was entirely on the art trip. She didn't even have her swimsuit with her.

Before she could respond, Jonathan replied to Oliver. 'I don't do wild swimming.'

Oliver grinned and a frown formed across his previously untroubled brow. 'Wild swimming?'

'Yes,' Oliver told him. 'Swimming in the sea or a river, outdoors in the wild. I don't do that. Sometimes I'll swim in a pool, though I'm more inclined to relax on a lounger by the poolside sipping a margarita.'

Oliver gestured to the beauty of the sun and the sea. 'What about taking your shoes off, rolling up the legs of your trews and going in for a wild paddle.'

The muscles in Jonathan's elegant jawline tensed. 'No, I gave up sloshing around in the sea when I was nine. But do continue to enjoy yourself wallowing in the shallows.'

Robin sensed that Oliver and Jonathan were rubbing each other up the wrong way, so she stepped in with a smile.

'I should've brought my swimsuit with me,' she said. 'The sea looks so tempting.'

'Perhaps next time you'll join me for a swim,' Oliver suggested.

Robin smiled. 'Yes, apparently we're in for a scorcher of a summer.'

'But the weather in Scotland can be so fickle,' said Jonathan. 'Though if you're used to roughing it, I'm sure you'll enjoy going for a dip regardless of the sleet, wind and rain.'

Avoiding a heated argument between the two men, Robin gestured to Jonathan's sketches.

'The cove and the coast are perfect for painting,' she said.

Oliver noticed she wasn't sketching anything. It was Jonathan with his mitts on the sketch pad and pencils.

'Are you sketching the cove for your textile art?' Oliver said to her.

'Eh, no, I forgot to bring an extra sketch pad with me,' she explained. 'I have a watercolour pad, but I prefer to sketch first.'

'I have one in my car, and pencils you can use,' Oliver offered.

Robin brightened at the offer.

Jonathan closed his sketch pad and stood up. 'We're heading for lunch, and then driving back to the castle.'

'The restaurant is really busy,' Oliver told them. 'You'll have to wait for a table. Or you may prefer something from the takeaway vans and stalls.'

'I don't do snack food,' said Jonathan. 'We planned to have a top cuisine lunch at the restaurant, so we will, even if we have to wait for a table.'

'I'd be happy to have a light snack,' said Robin.

Jonathan shook his head. 'No, let's stick to our plans — artwork and lunch, with strawberry and vanilla ice cream.'

Robin sensed the rivalry between the two men wasn't going to fade like the sunlight suddenly threatened to do, when it dimmed behind a solitary cloud in the sky. But then it emerged warm and bright again.

'Come on,' she said to Jonathan. 'Let's go and wait for a vacant table for lunch.'

Taking the hint that it was time for him to leave and let them get on with their day, Oliver smiled and started to walk back into the sea.

'I have something for you, Robin,' Oliver said, glancing over his shoulder.

'What is it?'

'It's a surprise. Drop by the shop when you're not busy,' said Oliver.

Robin nodded. 'I will. Any hint what it is you have for me?'

Oliver swithered and then decided to elaborate. 'A painting. A watercolour.'

Robin blinked. 'For me? You've painted something for me?'

Oliver nodded, smiled and then dived into the sea and swam back along the coast to where he'd left his shoes.

His shoes were still lying on the sand where he'd left them. He stepped into them, and walked up to the small esplanade. The restaurant was buzzing with customers. Robin and Jonathan were in for a long wait.

Back at his car, Oliver fetched a sketch pad and pencils from the boot. He rarely went anywhere without at least one pad and one pencil. There were three pads and several pencils to pick from. His car had them stashed in the glove compartment and other dookits, including one of the zip pockets of his duffel bag.

The sun was so warm he'd air dried by the time he'd reached his car, so he didn't fuss drying himself with his towel, not yet anyway. First, he took the pad and pencils over to where Robin and Jonathan were sitting outside the restaurant under the shade of the turquoise and white stripe awning, waiting for their number to be called for a vacant table.

Oliver smiled at Robin and shrugged his broad shoulders. 'Just in case you want to sketch the sea while you're sitting there.' He handed her the items.

Robin gladly accepted them. 'Thank you, Oliver. I appreciate it.'

Smiling at Robin and giving a curt nod to Jonathan, Oliver walked away to one of the snack vans. He bought a chip piece. Two thick cut slices of buttered bread were filled with fresh cooked chips, and garnished with tomato sauce and fried onions.

Robin watched him, feeling hungry and tempted to join him. But she didn't. Jonathan sneered, unimpressed by Oliver's food of choice.

Eating his snack, Oliver headed to his car. He gave himself a quick wipe down with the towel, put his clothes on and drove away from the cove feeling his heart twist as he saw Robin sitting sketching alongside Jonathan. Two artists drawing in tandem, and yet apart from everyone around them — all the people enjoying swimming in the sea, playing on the sand and making the most of the sunny day.

'Table for two,' one of the restaurant staff said to Robin and Jonathan.

Robin closed her sketch pad and stuffed it in her bag along with the pencils. Jonathan handed her his pad and pencils too, and she put them in the bag.

They were seated at a table near the window. Every table was occupied, and they'd landed lucky with a window view.

Robin studied the menu and ordered the vegetable pie with shortcrust pastry and minted new potatoes with bramble sauce.

Jonathan pondered his selection, finally deciding to settle for the seared salmon with a heather honey and lemon sauce drizzled over it, garnished with a green salad and a side order of sweet potato wedges.

Their lunch was served up swiftly.

Robin looked impressed. 'This is delicious,' she said, savouring the pie. 'The pastry is melt in the mouth scrumptious.'

Jonathan sampled his salmon and nodded. 'Very tasty.'

Robin continued to eat her lunch while Jonathan regaled tales of his artist exploits. She nodded on cue, and yet...his voice drifted into the background as she gazed out at the sea and dazzling white sand...and thought about Oliver. She rewound him striding out of the sea, taking her totally by surprise. He looked great. Handsome. She knew he was, but seeing him like this...well...

She didn't want to risk getting a broken heart. Oliver could be a heartbreaker, probably he was, and had been. He was sooo good looking. Not that she was looking. But Oliver was hard to ignore with his tall, fit build, dark brown hair and green eyes...

'...and after we finish lunch we should head back to the loch. I'd like to sketch it while the sun's out.'

Jonathan's words cut into her faraway thoughts, jarring her back to where she was.

'Yes,' Robin agreed. 'The loch looks wonderful in the sunlight. I love how the surface reflects the sky, taking on the colour of it, from stormy grey to summery blue.'

Strawberry and vanilla ice cream was served up to them.

Robin tasted a spoonful of the strawberry and nodded. 'I'm definitely a strawberry ice cream type.'

Jonathan sampled the vanilla, approving of the rich, classic ice cream.

Her mind drifted again to Oliver...what had he painted for her?

'...no trip to the seaside is complete without ice cream.' Jonathan's words broke into her thoughts.

'Yes,' she agreed, and then glanced out the window at the people enjoying going for a swim. 'Or without swimming in the sea.'

CHAPTER FOUR

Oliver jumped in the shower, washed the sand and sea water from himself, and then got dressed and went downstairs to his art shop. The day still had some afternoon sunlight in it, so he opened the front door to let it in.

Checking his website for orders, he'd only had a few and those were from online customers asking for more prints from his new collections, so they were easy to deal with.

His stomach rumbled, reminding him that he was firing on the fumes of a chip piece, so he made himself a cup of tea and took a bite of his snowball while contemplating his plan of action regarding Robin, and Jonathan.

Cake crumbs tumbled on to the kitchen table as he ate the snowball and drank his tea while scrolling through his laptop for any other information he could find about Jonathan, especially his artwork. He had talent, Oliver admitted, though it wasn't really to his taste. There was something lacking in all of Jonathan's paintings. And then he realised what was missing.

'Ah,' he mumbled to himself, leaning back and viewing Jonathan's paintings with a fresh perspective.

Finishing his tea, Oliver went through to the front shop and continued working on his night scene painting, feeling in the mood to work with the watercolours. There were times when the artistry flowed from his brush and he became lost in his painting, forgetting about the time.

When he finally looked up and gazed out the window, it appeared that the sun was in a pugilistic mood because it had barely dimmed, and even now in the late afternoon, it was fighting off giving way to the mellow glow of the approaching evening. Had he not known the time, he'd have been fooled into thinking it was midday. The local forecast had been right. This month was going to be a scorcher.

As a red car pulled up outside his shop, perhaps today was going to still be a scorcher too.

Robin stepped out of the car. Her hair shone like barely sugar in the sunlight. Oliver was particular about categorising the colour of Robin's hair. By all accounts, she was a strawberry blonde, and although he agreed in principal, the artist in him saw her in a whole different spectrum of almost white golden strands, with low lights of burnished amber and highlights of twenty–four carat brilliance. Barley sugar was the colour he thought about when he looked at Robin's beautiful, long hair. There were jars of the sweets in the window of the sweet shop opposite, made by Sylvia and her Aunt Muira. He'd even bought a poke of sweeties recently that included chunks of the barley sugar they made on the premises that could easily pass for pieces of amber. Yes, Robin was a barley sugar beauty — and now she was heading towards his shop.

Oliver's first instinct was delight, and then descended to dread as Jonathan decided to join her.

No, no, no! He felt the panic rush through him. The last thing he wanted was for Robin to come in looking for whatever gift he'd made for her — with Jonathan in tow.

Kicking himself for telling her at the cove, of course she'd be curious to find out what it was. She was bound to drop by on her way back from the coast. Obviously Jonathan was with her.

Before he could beat himself up for making a mistake, again, Robin breezed in through the open doorway, smiling at him, looking like she hadn't been anywhere near the shore. No wet hair from swimming, no sand on her pumps, nothing. But she did have a healthy glow on her cheeks, unless he was mixing that up with inner rage. He gave her the benefit of the doubt and smiled brightly, casually, as if he wasn't a man in a wind tunnel of trouble of his own making.

'Robin, come on in. Did you have a nice time at the cove?'

'I did,' she said, with an undertone that wasn't entirely convincing.

Jonathan walked in looking like he wouldn't want to own a shop like this. It was the first time Oliver had stood face to face with him, realising that Jonathan was as tall as he was. They eyeballed each other through forced, socially polite smiles.

'What a quaint little shop,' Jonathan said, trying and succeeding to take the edge off of Oliver's achievement of owning and running a thriving art shop business. He walked over to one wall where oil and acrylic paintings showed Oliver's talent in creating atmospheric Scottish landscapes and seascapes, and others depicting a town or city in the rain with the reflections from the shop windows and people walking along huddling from the downpour. Atmosphere was something that Oliver excelled at.

Paintings on the walls and on display included snow scenes, a foggy autumn day, a fresh spring morning, with large watercolour florals — roses, Scottish bluebells, forget–me–nots, foxgloves, pink lily of the valley, coral bells, cornflowers and Scottish thistle paintings — including exquisite butterflies, dragonflies, ladybirds and bees. And figurative pieces, from a single figure standing in the heart of the Highlands, to people hurrying along on stormy days. His range was wide, but bore his distinctive style.

No one seeing these paintings could deny Oliver's talent. Not even Jonathan.

Rather than give credit to Oliver, Jonathan ran a critical eye over the starry sky watercolour on the desk.

'Is this the main street?' Jonathan said, glancing out the window and comparing the view with the painting.

'Yes, it looked spectacular last night, so I took a few photos and started work on it,' Oliver explained.

'I'm sure it'll be nice when it's finished,' said Jonathan. His comment hung in the air like verbal poison.

Robin stepped in with the perfect antidote, dispersing the tension with the reason she was there.

'I can't stand the suspense,' Robin said to Oliver. 'You painted a watercolour for me. I'd love to see it.'

Oliver flicked a glance at Jonathan and then looked at her.

She got the message, realising he'd wanted to give her the gift privately.

But here they were, so rather than stall for time, Oliver went over to the portfolio, took the watercolour out and handed it to her.

Jonathan craned across to see what it was.

'My cottage,' she exclaimed, clearly delighted. 'You've painted my cottage!'

'I have a light cream frame that I'd be happy to put it in.'

Robin looked up at him. 'Would you? That would be great. I'd love to hang it in my living room.'

Jonathan gave no opinion on the cottage painting. Instead he looked at Robin. 'Do you ever want to try your hand at proper art?'

Robin frowned. 'Proper art?'

'Yes,' said Jonathan. 'Picking up a brush to paint oils on canvas, or actual watercolour paintings, rather than sticking and stitching pieces of fabric with embroidery thread to depict a landscape or sea scene.'

Robin blinked, feeling insulted and yet wondering if Jonathan intended to be so blunt.

'You could take an art course in it,' Jonathan suggested helpfully. 'If you're not confident in your artistic ability.'

Jonathan's first comment cut her to the bone. The second remark twisted the knife in deeper. Robin hadn't been prepared for such vitriol prettily wrapped as a pleasant remark.

The awkward silence dampened the happy mood.

Jonathan's remark rankled Oliver. 'What about you, Jonathan? Have you ever wanted to paint figures, people?'

Ruffled, but hiding it, Jonathan sneered at Oliver. 'I don't paint people. I'm not into figurative art.'

'Hmm,' said Oliver. 'Yes, I noticed that there are no people in your landscapes or any of your paintings. And no deer or sheep in the fields, no creatures in the flowers. No birds in the trees or the sky. Nothing with a beating heart. Not even a robin.'

Jonathan didn't have a suitable comeback, and Oliver filled the gap with a piece of helpful advice.

'You could take a course in figure painting,' Oliver told him, circling back to the remark Jonathan had made to Robin. 'If you're not confident in your artistic ability to paint people or creatures.'

Jonathan tried to smile as if unperturbed. He checked the time.

'We'd better be going if you want to show me the loch while the sun's still out,' Jonathan reminded Robin.

Robin smiled tightly at Jonathan. 'Yes, let's go.' She smiled back at Oliver. 'Thank you again for the painting. I love it.'

Oliver watched Robin leave with Jonathan and drive off in her car. She liked the painting. He was happy with that.

Taking the watercolour through to the back of his shop, he added a cream mounting board border to tidy up the edges of the painting and then framed it for her.

He'd just sat it up in his shop when Bradoch phoned him. He frowned, wondering if something was wrong as he took the call.

'Oliver, just to let you know that Gaven phoned to invite me to an impromptu party night at the castle,' said Bradoch. 'He's inviting a few local people to join the hotel guests. I mentioned to him that you would probably be interested in going, so he said you're welcome to pop along.'

'A party at the laird's castle? Tonight?' Oliver clarified, taken aback by the call.

'Yes. The hotel guests include Jonathan. Gaven's calling him to invite him to the party. It was mainly for the hotel guests, but he's including those in the self–catering cabins.'

'Jonathan will be there?'

'Yes, and as he's been with Robin all day, it's very likely he'll invite her to join him this evening. I thought if you went to the party, you could maybe dance with Robin.'

'Thanks for wangling an invitation for me,' Oliver told Bradoch.

'See you tonight then? Seven o'clock.'

'I'll be there.'

Oliver's plans for the evening had been to relax after the hectic day. Now he planned to get himself ready for a night at the castle, and a chance to dance with Robin.

Robin drove along the loch and stopped to show Jonathan the view.

52

Burnished sunlight shone across the smooth surface of the water, creating a scene that was beautifully picturesque. Rolling hills bordered it, with cottages, including her own, scattered on the hillsides. In the near distance at the far end of the loch was the road leading to the castle. The turrets peered over the hills, and in the opposite direction was the route to the main street. Everything was within walking distance or a short drive away.

The sky was mellowing, with bands of amber merging with the cloudless blue.

Robin sighed just looking at it. 'It's lovely, isn't it?'

Jonathan nodded, but seemed distracted by the distant hills. 'Is there a road up there? The loch's nice, but I'm not feeling the inspiration. What's at the top of the hillside? A view of the fields?'

Robin jolted out of her calm thoughts. 'Yes, farmland.' She started up the engine and drove off up the hillside. 'There's a place for cars to park that offers a fantastic view of the whole countryside.'

Jonathan perked up, looking out the window as they climbed higher until they reached the viewing area.

Robin parked the car. In front of them an expansive view, a patchwork of fields and countryside beyond. A romantic area high above the loch and the village main street. She didn't tell him that locally this was known as the kissing spot.

Robin stepped out and breathed in the fresh air.

Jonathan got out and took pictures with his phone. 'This is great. I like the patchwork of greens and barley yellows. I could work with this.'

As he held his phone, a call came through from the laird.

'Jonathan, there's a party at the castle this evening,' Gaven told him. 'I hope you can join us. Dinner, dancing, that sort of thing. It's been such a warm day I thought we'd make an evening of it.'

'I'd love to join you. A party sounds great. I should be finished the tour soon and heading back to the cabin.'

'See you around seven,' said Gaven.

'Yes.' Jonathan finished the call.

'That was the laird. There's a party at the castle tonight. I've been invited,' Jonathan told Robin.

'The parties at the castle are always great fun.' Her words hung in the warm, still air.

Jonathan focussed again on the view, took a few more pictures, checked he had what he needed and then smiled at Robin.

'Okay, it's be quite a day, but I'd like to head back to the castle now to get ready for the party.'

Without further discussion about the invitation, they got into the car and Robin drove them the short distance to the castle and dropped Jonathan off outside his cabin. It was a stylish, luxury cabin set within the trees on the castle's estate.

Jonathan got out of the car and then leaned in and smiled at her.

'Thank you for taking the time to give me the tour. Could I rip my sketches out of your pad before you go?'

Slightly flummoxed, and yet thinking why should Jonathan invite her to the party, she tried not to be miffed. He wasn't obliged to spend the evening with her just because they'd had a day out.

Reaching into the back seat for the sketch pad, she handed it to him.

Jonathan carefully extracted his sketches of the cove and handed it back to her.

Smiling, he gave a cheery wave and headed into the cabin.

Robin drove off, wondering why she felt slighted, and headed home to her cottage.

She parked her car and stepped out, breathing in the early evening air, noticing that the day was mellowing fast. Her favourite view calmed her senses, and she tried to shake off the feeling of having been pleasantly dismissed from Jonathan's company.

Digging out her keys from her bag, she unlocked the door and went inside, closing it firmly against the world that sometimes crushed the breath from her.

But then she thought about Oliver, and the painting as she walked into her living room, feeling the homeliness wrap around her, the familiar glow of the sunlight streaming through the windows. She pictured where she'd hang the painting — on the wall near her work desk where she could admire it.

After a shower to wash away the sense of the day, she put on comfy casuals — pale grey lounge trousers and a pink and white top, and padded around in her slippers to make dinner.

She checked the freezer for something easy to cook. A half pizza with a generous topping of cheese, cherry tomatoes, red, yellow and green peppers, and red onion looked tasty. She popped it in the oven and rustled up a salad to go with it. And a pot of tea.

She opened the kitchen door to let the garden air waft in, and sat down at the kitchen table to eat her dinner.

Rewinding the events of the day, she kept circling back to Oliver. The painting of her cottage was a wonderful surprise, and she was looking forward to hanging it in her living room.

She tried and failed not to think about Oliver wading out of the sea, his lean muscled body glistening wet, and that handsome face of his smiling at her. The thought of him, all tall, broad shouldered, fit and sexy set her senses alight.

The kitchen was already hot from the heat of the oven without her thinking about playing with fire, because that's what it would be. Oliver was a potential heartbreaker. No way was she putting her heart in jeopardy.

After eating her dinner and clearing away the dishes, she stepped outside into her back garden. The air was calm, just what she needed. She breathed it in and sipped her mug of tea.

If someone gave her a choice — attend the party at the castle with Jonathan...or...relax in her pretty cottage, snuggle up and enjoy an evening of sewing the seascape she had in mind...she would select a night in at her cottage. No hesitation.

She pictured using a light wash of aquamarine on pieces of cotton fabric to depict the sea, and cerulean for the sky. Distant islands far out at sea would be hinted at.

As stars started to appear in the twilight sky, Robin went inside and through to the living room to make a start on the seascape. She rummaged through her fabric stash for the pieces she needed to represent the cove and the sea. Part of the joy of her textile art was playing around with gorgeous pieces of fabric and selecting the embroidery thread from the wonderful range of thread she had. New colours in aquamarine and green tones along with bright yellows and pinks, had arrived recently and she was looking forward to using them.

Oliver put on a white shirt, blue silk tie and a dark grey suit, got into his car, and drove to the castle for the party night.

As he drove along the edge of the loch, he noticed the lights were still on in Robin's cottage. He was a bit early. She'd be getting ready for the party, so he fought the urge to pop over and offer her a lift. Robin had her own car. And the last thing she'd need was him dropping by when she was getting dressed. Besides, maybe Jonathan was due to arrive, pick her up and drive her there, like a real date.

Pushing this scenario aside as it caused his guts to twist at the thought of Jonathan being her date for the party, Oliver drove on, heading along the road leading to the castle. He'd meet Robin at the party — and ask her to dance with him.

He'd wrapped her painting up and put it in the boot of his car, to give it to her later, if the appropriate moment presented itself during the evening. If not, he'd give it to her another time.

Driving up into the hills, he paused and pulled over to admire the view, and to settle himself. He was excited to have the chance to dance with Robin, but anxious that perhaps she wasn't interested in him. Trying to boost his confidence, he sat there for a short while gazing out at the calming view.

Then he drove along the road leading to the castle. He glimpsed the turrets through the trees, and drove through the wide open gates that led up to the front entrance. The car park was busy, but he found a parking spot.

Breathing in the night air as he walked to the front entrance, steeling himself at the prospect of seeing Robin enjoying herself with Jonathan, he searched the faces for her. He saw Jonathan standing at the function room bar ordering what looked to be a cocktail for himself. One drink.

Where was Robin, Oliver wondered, intending to ask Gaven when he saw him, or Jessy or one of the other guests from the local community.

'Good evening, Oliver,' Gaven said to him.

Oliver glanced round and saw the laird smiling at him. 'Thank you for inviting me this evening.'

'My pleasure.'

'Have you seen Robin?' said Oliver.

'No, but Jonathan's over at the bar. He'll probably know where she is. Perhaps she's just fashionably late,' Gaven suggested, and then excused himself as he was needed to deal with a hotel guest at the reception.

Oliver looked around. There was no sign of Robin. Fashionably late or not.

CHAPTER FIVE

Robin opened the living room window to let the air from the garden into her cottage. It was a lovely warm night and she eased off the tension of the day. Her textile art seascape was starting to look great. The embroidery thread she'd selected to stitch the layers of blue and green chiffon to the background cotton fabric, created the texture of the waves drifting on to the white sand.

Wandering through to the kitchen to make a cup of tea, she decided instead to have a glass of ginger, sparkling lemonade, with ice cream. Scooping a spoonful of vanilla ice cream into a tall glass, she topped it up with lemonade from the fridge. Then she used a long spoon to stir her glass of ginger and ice cream, and sat outside on a garden chair to enjoy it.

The evening air was so still with barely a breeze, and the fragrance from the flowers in her back garden was heady with the scent of roses, jasmine and night–scented stock.

Her view from the garden was nothing but hills, like soft velvet in shades of green with splashes of purple, lilac and white heather. Perched halfway up the gentle hillside, there was no one to look down on her, ensuring an excellent level of privacy.

But she assumed that her adventure with Jonathan would already have been relayed by the well–meaning gossipmongers. She was bound to have been seen at the busy cove with Jonathan and having lunch with him at the restaurant. There were no secrets, or very few, in the close–knit community, especially among the members of the crafting bee. Etta was everyone's go–to for the latest gossip, and Jessy was the direct line to everything that was going on with the laird and the castle.

Etta often met up for a morning cup of tea and scones at Bradoch's bakery with other members of the bee, especially those owning shops nearby like Aileen with her quilt shop and Sylvia from the sweet shop. They'd blether about the latest gossip. Robin often joined them for a cuppa and chit–chat.

Sighing heavily, she pictured being the topic of gossip, but that wouldn't last, and soon someone else would be in the spotlight.

For a moment she wondered if Jonathan was having fun at the party, then immediately brushed all thoughts of him aside. Jonathan was, if she was being kind, an acquired taste, but he'd left a bitterness that she found hard to erase. In the morning, she planned to get on with her own work, and mentally cast her tour guide badge into the past.

With Jonathan monopolising her time and her sketch book, she aimed to head back to the cove and take her textile art with her to compare it to the colours of the sea and sky. And sketch from real life. Photos were great, but she liked to draw while soaking in the atmosphere. And seeing all those people in swimming had put her in the notion of looking out her swimsuit and going for a dook in the sea while she was there. With only herself to answer to, she planned to set off in the morning to the cove.

She sipped her ice cream drink and enjoyed the evening air while making her plans. The night sky, sparkling with stars, promised another warm day, so she wanted to make the most of it. According to the forecast, it was one of those times when the summer was going to be a scorcher.

Finishing her drink, she went back inside to get on with her artwork.

The turquoise blue embroidery thread was a lovely stranded cotton. She threaded her needle with two strands and used outline stitches to embroider the distant islands. Deep blue strands of embroidery thread and back stitches added to the impression of boats sailing along the coast. She'd cut pieces of solid blue and red cotton fabric and stitched them on to create the sails, and scraps of white fabric for the hulls, leaving the edges of the fabric raw.

Every now and then, as she sat in her living room, embroidering the seascape, she thought about Oliver striding from the sea, smiling, so fit and handsome. She wondered what he was doing this evening. Probably working on his paintings. Apparently, he often painted well into the night when he was painting a new piece of artwork. The watercolour scene she'd seen earlier in his shop looked wonderful, even when it wasn't finished.

Oliver approached Jessy. She was working at the castle's reception desk.

She smiled, seeing him walk over to her from the party in the function room.

'I'm looking for Robin,' he said. 'Have you seen her?'

'No, but she's probably running a bit late. You know what it's like. Hair, makeup, trying to decide what dress to wear.'

Oliver understood and yet...a niggling doubt was bothering him. 'Gaven did invite her, didn't he?'

Jessy thought for a moment. 'Not personally, no. But he definitely phoned Jonathan while he was with Robin, and invited him to the party night. Jonathan is bound to have asked her to go with him. Why wouldn't he? I heard they got along so well. They had a trip to the cove and they were sketching the scenery together, and then he took her for lunch at the lovely restaurant.'

Oliver waited, wondering if Jessy would mention that he was there too. But no. Nothing was said about him being at the cove or swimming in the sea. Not even a hint that he'd painted a watercolour for her either. Those snippets of gossip clearly hadn't circulated yet.

'What's wrong, Oliver? You're looking pensive,' said Jessy.

'Can I ask you something?' he said in a confiding tone.

Jessy nodded.

'What do you think about Jonathan?'

'Well...' she took a deep breath. 'Just between you and me?'

'Yes,' he assured her.

'He's very suave, tall and handsome, a man that most women would find enticing. But I think he's got a fancy for Robin. And she was all smiles when they drove off this morning from the castle after breakfast. They seemed to be getting along like a house on fire.' She nodded thoughtfully. 'There was certainly a spark between them.'

Oliver's heart twisted with every word.

'To tell you the truth, Oliver, I think there could be a romance blossoming with Jonathan and Robin.'

This was the last thing he wanted to hear.

'I appreciate you telling me,' he said.

'There was a time when we all thought that you had a wee fancy for Robin, but obviously we were wrong,' Jessy told him.

He almost confessed that they'd been right. But if it was true that Robin liked Jonathan, even though he hadn't seen any spark of attraction between the two of them, then he'd only cause ructions. He needed to think how to handle the situation, and right now, his mind was preoccupied wondering where Robin was, and if she was going to be at the party. If not, he wouldn't hang around long, especially as Jonathan was smirking at him.

'Was there something you wanted from Robin?' Jessy said to Oliver.

'No, I thought she'd be at the party, invited by Jonathan,' he explained. 'I have something to give to her.'

'I'll tell her when I see her,' Jessy promised, and then had to excuse herself to attend to the hotel guests.

Oliver walked back into the function room, trying not to look at Jonathan, but it was difficult as he was now extolling the benefits of taking an artist's break at the castle to a group of party guests.

Standing at the edge of the dance floor, searching the faces for any sign of Robin, Oliver inadvertently got pulled into one of the Scottish reels by enthusiastic revellers, and danced three rounds before managing to escape.

Back in the reception area, a safe distance from further jigging, Gaven approached him.

'Robin's not coming to the party,' Gaven told him.

'Why not?'

'My mistake. I didn't invite her. I assumed Jonathan would bring her as his date.' He shrugged. 'But he didn't ask Robin.'

Bradoch approached them and joined in the conversation. 'I thought he'd invite her too. Jessy told me a couple of minutes ago that she asked Jonathan why he hadn't invited Robin.'

'What did he say?' said Oliver.

'He said he's only just arrived for his holiday, and he's not looking to get involved with anyone. He doesn't want to be tied down.'

Bradoch and Gaven seemed unimpressed with Jonathan's attitude, even though they understood that he preferred to remain free to do what he wanted.

But Oliver's heart soared.

Before Oliver could discuss the ramifications of this revelation, the castle's head chef came hurrying over, wearing an askew white hat and a perturbed expression. 'Excuse me, Gaven, but one of the tables has asked for baked Alaska for their pudding. It's not on the menu. I offered them our popular spotted dick as a tasty alternative, but they're having none of it. Could you come and talk them? I've a rough puff pastry pie in the oven and I need to rustle up more sausages.'

'Yes, I'll handle the guests,' Gaven said to the chef. 'You go back and attend to your sausages in the kitchen.' He looked at Oliver and Bradoch. 'Excuse me.'

They nodded, and Gaven strode off. It was his fault that the staff were extra busy. He'd landed them with the last minute party night, but he got on well with his staff and everyone mucked in.

'Come on, Bradoch,' a woman called over to him. 'You're missing out on the dancing.'

'You go,' Oliver said to Bradoch. 'I think I'll head for home.'

Bradoch nodded and went back to join the party.

Oliver headed out into the night, got into his car and drove off.

The short drive took him back to the loch, the surface smooth as dark glass in the gloaming.

He slowed down, opened the window and breathed in the calm atmosphere. The loch was picture perfect, and he made a mental note to paint it. He'd always meant to, but there were invariably other projects on his slate and so he'd yet to do a watercolour of it. Or oil, or perhaps acrylic. Maybe he'd paint a couple of pictures of the loch in different styles. It certainly merited being featured as part of his collections.

The rolling hills that bordered the loch were the ideal background, and it crossed his mind to paint a night–time scene, atmospheric with the deep, inky blue sky, glittering with stars and the silver white moon, fading down to the loch.

He'd include flowers in the foreground to add depth to the scene, and to emphasise the beauty of the area. Roses sprang to mind, and Scottish bluebells, thistles, cosmos, blue daisies, foxgloves, cornflowers, coral bells, heliotrope and forget–me–nots. Flowers were his forte, along with butterflies, bees and dragonflies flitting about them.

And he'd paint the cottages that were scattered around the hillside. There was Etta's cottage with its well–established garden, and Penny's and the one belonging to Neil the goldsmith.

Looking across the loch he saw Robin's cottage. His favourite. Traditional, with its whitewashed walls and a floral garden guarding it on all sides with its scented beauty.

The lights were still on.

He paused and considered what to do. It wasn't that late. He'd left the party early, so he decided to drive over and give her the painting.

The plan seemed straightforward, but as he parked at the bottom of the hillside, fetched the painting from the boot of his car and then walked up to her cottage, his heart was pounding nervously. What would go wrong now? He couldn't help feel anxious, because his latest efforts to talk to Robin had been thwarted.

Telling himself to buck up, he knocked on her door and stood there, holding the painting, still carefully wrapped, and was at least glad that he was well–dressed in his suit.

Robin was sitting in the living room, working on her seascape, when she heard someone at the front door. She wasn't expecting anyone, and rarely had visitors at this time of night, so she peeked out the window and saw Oliver standing there.

Hurrying through to the hall, she opened the door. 'Oliver!' She sounded surprised to see him.

'I hope I'm not interrupting anything,' he said.

'No, come in, I was working on my new seascape.' She led him through to the living room, impressed by how handsome he looked in his suit.

He unwrapped the painting and handed it to her. 'I thought you'd be at the party at the castle. I planned to give you the painting there.'

She smiled when she saw how beautifully he'd framed it. 'Thank you. This looks wonderful.' She walked over to where she planned to hang it on the wall and held it up. 'It'll look perfect there. I'll hang it up in the morning.'

'I'd be happy to help you now,' he offered.

'Great. What do you need?'

'Do you have a hammer?'

'Yes, there's one in the hall cupboard.' She went through to get it.

He unclipped the fixings on the back of the picture frame. 'I added fixings for you. It'll be easy to hang up.'

Robin came back and handed him the hammer.

Oliver went over to the wall and hung it up in minutes, clearly used to this sort of thing. 'There you go.' He stepped back to check that it was hanging straight.

She smiled and admired it on the wall. 'I love it. I really do. Thank you for painting it.' Though she still didn't know why he'd done this.

'I'd been painting various shops in the main street, as I'm sure you know, and I wanted to try my hand at painting one of the local cottages. I've always liked the look of this cottage, so...I painted it.' This was true. He just didn't add that he had a crush on her and hoped that the gift would show how much he liked her.

'I was going to put the kettle on for a cup of tea. Would you like a cup?' she offered him.

'Yes, that would be great.'

Robin went through to the kitchen, and he had a look around, gazing down at the piece of textile art on her table. 'Your seascape is lovely. I like the textures you've created with the fabric and stitches. Is that embroidery thread?'

'Yes,' she called through to him, as she filled the kettle and set the cups up. 'I embroider a lot of my artwork.'

He wandered through to the kitchen and stood in the doorway watching her prepare the tea.

Her heart reacted seeing his tall stature and broad shoulders fill the doorway.

'You're very talented, Robin.'

A blush started to form across her cheeks from the effects of seeing him standing there, coupled with the compliment.

'I don't mean to embarrass you,' he said.

'No, I'm fine, just feeling the heat of the day and the night,' she lied.

'It was a scorcher of a day.'

'I'm heading back to the cove tomorrow, on my own, taking my artwork with me — and maybe my swimsuit. Seeing you in swimming has put me in the mood to go for a dook.' And thinking about him in his trunks caused her to blush even more.

She opened the kitchen door. 'It's such a gorgeous night.' She breathed in the evening air.

He walked over and stood beside her, gazing out at the garden.

She barely came up to his shoulders.

'That's the one thing I miss living above the shop,' he said. 'Not having a garden to step out on to. My shop garden is fine, but one day I plan to have a house, one of the converted farmhouses or a cottage, if I can find one as lovely as this.' He glanced around. 'It's well–built, made to last.'

'That's what I love about it too. It feels reliable, sturdy, even on stormy days when the wind is blowing a hooley, the traditional build of it makes me feel safe and protected.' She shrugged. 'Maybe that says more about me than the cottage.'

His beautiful green eyes glanced down at her. 'Maybe it does, but it sounds ideal to me.'

The kettle clicked off, and she smiled at him and then went over to make the tea.

'Would you like something to eat?' she offered.

Oliver hesitated.

'Did you have dinner at the castle?'

'No, I was...too busy.' Looking for her. 'I was talking to Gaven and Bradoch, and Jessy.'

'What's the latest gossip?'

70

Oliver smiled. 'Jessy seemed to think that a romance was brewing between you and Jonathan.'

The teaspoon she was holding rattled against one of the cups. 'No, definitely not!'

'You know what the local gossip is like,' he said, trying to sound calm while feeling the opposite. Her reaction gave him hope.

'I do, but Jessy, and I'm assuming some of the other bee members like Etta, have got their wires crossed this time.'

'And last time too.'

'Oh, what did they get wrong last time?' She gestured for him to sit down at the kitchen table for his tea.

He sat down and helped himself to the milk, stirring it in, while buying time, trying to think how to word his reply.

'Was it scandal, or meddling in matchmaking, or...I don't know...romance?'

'Yes.' He sipped his tea.

'Which one?'

'They seemed to think that I liked you, then they decided that I didn't,' he told her. And then held his breath while his heart pounded, worried he'd said too much, and worried he'd said too little.

Robin blinked and looked at him across the table. 'What option did the gossip get wrong?' She tried to keep her voice level, while feeling a rush of excitement.

Come on, tell her the truth, speak up, he urged himself.

A knock on the front door startled both of them and curtailed their conversation.

'Are you expecting anyone?' Oliver said, wondering if Jonathan had been invited.

'No.' She got up and went through to peek out the window.

CHAPTER SIX

The tall, blond–haired figure of Fyn, the flower shop owner, smiled in at Robin through the window as he stood outside on the doorstep. His tall stature, unruly blond hair and handsome face with light blue eyes was lit up by the wall lantern.

He often wore jeans and denim shirts like the ones he was wearing, with the sleeves rolled up as if always ready to tackle his work. Fyn was single, early thirties, and although he'd dated one of the local women in the past, he'd yet to find someone to settle down with. But like Oliver, he lived in hope.

Fyn owned the flower shop in the main street. He sometimes gave Robin scatterings from his cut flowers to use for sketching floral designs for her textile art. His smiling and handsome face indicated that there was nothing wrong, but he'd never been to her cottage before.

'It's Fyn,' Robin said to Oliver and went to let him in.

'Is Oliver here?' Fyn thumbed behind him. 'I saw his car parked at your cottage and wondered if I could talk to him for a moment.'

'Yes, he's here, come on in.' She welcomed Fyn in and led him through to the living room.

Fyn smiled when he saw Oliver. 'I hope I'm not interrupting your evening.' He noticed that Oliver was smartly dressed in his suit, while Robin wore comfy casuals.

'No, I was just dropping off a painting for Robin.' Oliver indicated towards the painting on the wall.

Fyn looked at it and nodded. 'A lovely painting of your cottage, Robin.' And then he spoke to Oliver. 'It's your paintings I wanted to talk to you about. I popped by your shop earlier today, but you were closed. I left a message on your website, but I haven't heard back, so when I saw your car as I was driving by, I thought I might speak to you for a minute.'

'Sorry for not responding to your message,' Oliver told him. 'It's been a hectic day, and night.'

'That's okay, I have days like that myself,' said Fyn. 'I've been helping my brother out at the farm this evening.'

Fyn often helped out at his family's farm, one of the farms in the local area. His parents ran the farm, with the help of his brother, Gare, who'd opted for vegetable farming rather than flowers as a career. They got on well as a family and were supportive of Fyn's flower shop. Gare was younger than Fyn by a year and bore the same fit build and blond hair.

'What was it you wanted to talk to me about my paintings?' said Oliver.

'It's about those beautiful big flower paintings in your window display. I'd like one for my shop. I think it'll brighten up the wall behind the counter. I gave the walls a lick of white paint last week to freshen them up for the summer, but I put photos of it up on my website and I feel there's something missing. I've plenty of real flowers on display, but I'd love one of your large watercolours with the close–up views of flowers. They're stunning paintings, Oliver. But I don't know what one to buy. They're all lovely. So I'm looking for a bit of advice as well.'

'I tell you what, I'll give you the main one on display. The one with a whole mix of flowers with bees and butterflies,' Oliver suggested. 'Hang that up and see if it suits you. Then I'll give you one of the others in exchange. Hang each one for a day or two, and see what suits you.'

Fyn brightened. 'That's very kind of you. And I wondered if you have any wee watercolours of individual flowers — a rose, sunflower, cornflower, various types.'

'Yes, I have a portfolio stuffed to the gunnels with single florals. They're not framed or anything like that. They're just paintings I've done of the structure, how many petals the flower has, the type of leaves, that sort of thing, so when I'm painting the larger compositions I get it right. You can have a look through those. You'll know what you want better than me. I've everything from asters, bluebells, cosmos and daisies working my way through the alphabet to violets, wisteria, yarrow and zinnia.'

'Great. I appreciate it,' said Fyn. 'I want the shop looking tip–top. That's where I'm going now, to fit a new pale blue roller blind to the front window so the shop will look nice, like a summer sky.'

'Do you want a hand?' Oliver offered. 'I'm heading back to my shop. Two pairs of hands and all that.'

Fyn glanced at Robin and then at Oliver. 'I don't want to cut your visit here short.'

'I was due to leave soon,' said Oliver. 'Robin has her seascape to work on.'

Fyn leaned over for a look. 'That's really gorgeous,' he told her. 'I love the colours. It reminds me of the cove.'

Robin smiled, delighted. 'It is the cove! My version of it anyway.'

'You've got a great eye for colour,' Oliver agreed, and then got ready to go. 'Okay, I'll let you get on. I'm glad you like the cottage painting.'

'I love it,' she said.

Oliver and Fyn headed out to their cars. Robin stood in the doorway, lit up by the glow of the lantern, and waved them off.

Standing for a moment, she gazed out at the loch, breathing in the calm feeling of the night, then went inside and closed the door to the world, made herself a cup of tea and worked into the wee small hours on her textile art.

'Robin's nice, isn't she?' Fyn said to Oliver as they put the roller blind up in the front window of the flower shop. Oliver's art shop was across the street, so it was handy for him to help.

'She is,' Oliver agreed. He held the blind steady while Fyn drilled the fittings to the window frame.

'Was that a spark I sensed between the two of you?'

Oliver adjusted one end of the blind so that it could be fitted well. 'I think so. Hopefully not just on my part.'

'No, I saw the way Robin was looking at you, all suave and sophisticated in your suit.'

Oliver laughed.

'Were you out on business?' said Fyn.

'No.' He gave Fyn the short course of the day's events, culminating in the party night at the castle.

'This Jonathan sounds like an acquired taste.'

'That's a very tactful way of putting it.'

They both laughed, and then taking an end each, they slotted the blind across the large front window.

Fyn tested that it rolled up and down smoothly. 'Like butter. Thanks for your help.'

'Nae bother.'

Agreeing that Fyn would come over in the morning and pick up the large watercolour painting, so he could view the colours in the daylight, and have a look through the floral portfolio, Oliver went to leave.

Fyn said something before Oliver left. 'As a single man with no girlfriend of my own, I know I've got a cheek offering you advice on your love life, but for what it's worth...if you like Robin, don't drag your heels this time. Tell her. Ask her out.'

'That's sound advice, thanks.' Then Oliver laughed.

'What is it?'

'The reason I didn't ask Robin out a while ago was because I'd heard a rumour that she was dating one of the local farmers. Gossip gone wrong, but I thought she was dating your brother, Gare.'

Fyn guffawed. 'No, he's as unlucky as we are when it comes to the ladies. But can I tell him? He'll be flattered.'

Oliver shrugged. 'Why not. It's old gossip, but it's why I didn't ask Robin for a date sooner. I thought she had a boyfriend.'

'All the more reason not to drag your heels this time,' Fyn reminded him.

Oliver nodded and smiled, then he walked over to his shop and went upstairs to get ready for bed.

He hung his suit up in the wardrobe and then stood wearing only his boxers gazing out his bedroom window — thinking about Robin.

Robin worked on the seascape, embroidering it with several shades of blues and greens with accents of amber and ochre for the coast, and white for the sand. Stem stitch in green tones created the grass on the dunes, and dashes of bright colours made the thistles and other florals look lovely, especially as she used crewel wool to embroider the thistles for a soft textured effect.

And all the while she kept glancing up and admiring the cottage painting.

Finally finishing her work for the evening, she tidied up her desk, leaving the seascape on a table, planning to put any little extra on it in the morning.

But looking at the seascape and then at the cottage painting, she had an idea.

Popping outside, she took photos of the front of her cottage in the glow of the night, with the starry sky stretching into the distance. She checked the images. Just what she had in mind.

Hurrying back inside, she sketched a rough outline of her cottage, the flowers in the garden and the skyline.

Excitement wiped away any weariness, and she rummaged through her fabric stash to find scrap pieces to create a textile artwork of her cottage.

She painted dark blue watercolours across the night sky, intending to add couched strands of metallic gold thread for the stars and the moon.

White cotton for the whitewashed cottage was layered with pieces of grey for the window frames and warm yellow to create a glow from the lights inside.

The artwork started to take shape, and she kept adding pieces to make the door, the garden flowers, and embroidered the roof with crewel wool making it look textured.

It was getting late, and with the basis of her new cottage artwork done, she turned the lights off in the living room and went to bed.

Lying there, thinking of the events of the day, the best parts where Oliver was involved, the moonlight streamed through her window and across her bed, making her feel like she was tucked up safe and cosy in a real life painting of her own.

Oliver breathed in the bright sunny morning as he opened the front door of his shop to let the warm air in.

He was taking the large watercolour he'd promised to give to Fyn out of the window display, when Fyn came walking across from his flower shop.

'Morning,' Fyn said, seeing Oliver lift the painting off the stand.

'Nice timing.' Oliver handed the painting to Fyn. 'Here you are. There are fixings taped to the back of the frame for putting it up on the wall.'

Fyn held the painting and admired the colours in the daylight. 'This is a corker. Thanks for letting me have it. It's likely that this is the one I'll buy, but I appreciate you giving me a chance to see the different ones in my shop. I'll be recommending your art to my customers.'

Oliver smiled. 'Cheers. And I have that portfolio of small watercolour flowers through the back.' He went to get it.

Fyn rested the large painting on the counter. The white frame enhanced the colours of the gorgeous flowers. He glanced around the shop and saw a set of four small floral watercolours hanging up and went over for a closer. They had creamy white frames and borders to match.

'Oliver, I like these,' Fyn called through to him.

Bringing the portfolio through, Oliver wondered what had interested Fyn.

'These are exactly what I was looking for.' Fyn admired the sunflower, red rose, purple thistle and blue cornflower.

'Take the set with you as well,' Oliver told him.

'No, I'm definitely buying these, and one of the big paintings too, when I decide which one.'

'Settle up with me later when you've made up your mind.' Oliver proceeded to unhook the four small floral paintings and put them carefully into a bag. 'There you are.'

Delighted with the paintings, Fyn thanked him again, and then carried the paintings over to his shop.

With a gap in his window display, Oliver wondered what he'd fill it with. He'd several floral watercolours hanging up in the shop, or tucked away. Selecting a painting that looked like a summer garden, he put that in the window, and then stood outside to check that it looked okay.

Etta, Aileen and Sylvia sat at one of the tables at the window of Bradoch's bakery having early morning tea and scones with strawberry jam and cream. The gossip from Jessy at the castle merited a chit–chat.

'And Jessy said that Oliver turned up at the castle looking for Robin,' Etta told them. 'But Jonathan hadn't even invited her to the party, even after they'd had a day out at the cove and lunch there at the restaurant.'

The details were discussed while they sipped their tea and ate the scones.

Aileen shook her head. 'That wasn't very nice of him.'

Etta shrugged. 'According to Jessy, he's not interested in getting involved with anyone while he's here on holiday. But he could've invited her, just as friends.'

'Why was Oliver looking for Robin at the party?' Sylvia said to Etta.

'He'd brought something with him, he wanted to give it to her,' Etta explained. 'We don't know what it was. Probably something to do with his art. But Jessy said that Oliver was looking very smart and handsome in his suit.'

'Bradoch said he had a great time at the party,' said Aileen.

'Yes, Gaven's party nights are usually fun,' said Etta. 'But Jessy says she's advised Gaven not to pair Robin with Jonathan again, and he agrees. So there should be no trouble from him for Robin.'

The women agreed this was best. Jonathan could find someone else to be his personal tour guide if he needed one.

Bradoch was busy serving customers coming in for their morning rolls and bread. He could overhear the threesome's conversation and was tempted to add a few details, but he was distracted when he noticed Oliver outside his art shop across the street. He was on his phone — and dancing up and down.

Bradoch blinked. 'What's Oliver doing dancing in the street?'

Etta, Aileen and Sylvia looked out the window. So too did a couple of customers.

Oliver's antics were quite pronounced. Something, the phone call perhaps, had made him jump for joy.

Bradoch and the women started laughing.

'Look at him go!' said Sylvia.

'Something's made him happy,' Etta surmised. 'He's still on his phone, so it must be great news.'

Aileen giggled. 'I didn't know Oliver could dance like that.'

Bradoch finished serving the customers, and hurried to open the door.

'Oliver!' Bradoch shouted over to him.

Oliver waved, finished taking the call, put the phone in his pocket and came running across to the bakery. 'Sorry for the impromptu jigging. It was, eh...news about an order for my paintings.'

'It must have been some news to make you dance like that,' said Bradoch, as they stood at the bakery's front door. Then he lowered his voice. 'I thought maybe it was to do with Robin. That she'd agreed to have a date with you.'

'I wish. No, it was a business call, about my art,' Oliver said truthfully. 'Nothing special,' he lied.

And then giving Bradoch and the ladies a cheery wave, Oliver bounded back over to his art shop and disappeared inside.

CHAPTER SEVEN

Oliver could barely contain his delight and surprise at the great phone call from his agent. He'd had the same art agent for years, and usually his calls to Oliver involved deals like the recent one to create a collection of paintings for a home decor company.

But Oliver had sent his agent something else — a picture book that he'd illustrated with beautiful watercolour art. He'd written five hundreds words of a story to go with it. In essence, a complete picture book — artwork and editorial.

His agent said he'd submit it for consideration to a book publisher in London. Oliver tucked his hopes in his back pocket and pushed on with his regular artwork — paintings. A book deal was a dream he'd had for years, and he never expected he'd receive a three–book deal!

Now he had to wait for his agent to call back. He'd phoned Oliver with the news that his book had been accepted, with two other books in the series required, and what type of deal it was. Oliver agreed to the offer, so his agent had to call the publishing company and then phone Oliver back again.

He was tense and elated. A jarring mix. Since he was a young boy, he'd loved picture books. His parents bought them for him, knowing he enjoyed looking at the pictures, the artwork and reading the story. As he grew up, and realised he had a talent for art, that was nurtured by his school teachers and his parents, he continued to love picture books, finding joy in the art, wishing that one day he'd create a picture book of his own and have it published. Now his dream had come true, when he'd almost forgotten about it. For although he knew his agent had a copy of the artwork and the words, time had passed and he'd become busy with other things.

Oliver jumped with excitement when his phone rang.

'Oliver,' his agent said, sounding delighted. 'The publishers are happy that you've accepted the deal. And they now want the original artwork for the book.'

'I have the originals tucked safely in a portfolio. I'll send it direct to you in Edinburgh, or should I send it by courier to the publishers?'

'No, bring it with you. The publishers want to meet you, so you'll have to pop down to London,' his agent told him. 'Drive to Edinburgh this evening, stay overnight at my house. We'll go over the contact and discuss our plans for the meeting. Then we'll catch the first flight to London in the morning.'

'Go to London tomorrow morning?' Oliver's mind whirred with the unexpected trip.

'Yes. I'll book a hotel near the publishers and arrange a late morning meeting with them. That's what they've suggested.'

'Is it really necessary? I mean, can't I just send the original art? They have the editorial I wrote.'

'Oliver,' his agent said firmly. 'This is the chance of a lifetime. Your dream come true. Not only that, they're offering you a three–book deal, so yes, it's absolutely necessary.'

'Of course, yes,' Oliver conceded. 'My mind's still in a whirl.'

'I understand. I'm as delighted as you are. I loved the story, the artwork, the characters, it's such a wonderful book. I hoped they'd see in you what I see, a real talent. Now, do what you need to deal with your shop, let your customers know you'll be away for a couple of days.'

'Two days?'

'Three at the most. It depends on whether the publishers want to have a second meeting with you. They're talking about pushing this title forward at speed. Usually, it would take a year at least to get something like this ready for publishing. But with the finished artwork you've done, and the story, plus you've painted the cover, well...it's almost ready to go.'

'When are they thinking of publishing it?' said Oliver.

'They'd like to have it out for Christmas.'

'That's fast.'

'I know, but you've already done the work, to artwork finished level, and they don't want to alter any of the story. They love the whole package. And they want two more in the series following on with the same characters. Other little tales of what the bees, wasps, butterflies and the greenflies are up to in the cottage garden by the watery loch. I'm sure you've got another two stories in you. You spoke to me about another story set in the summer garden, another adventure for the wee creatures. But that artwork of yours, those watercolour flowers, that's what they want you to do again.'

'I can do that,' Oliver assured him.

'That's settled then. I'll see you later. Phone when you're on your way. Bring a sharp suit and tidy clothes for the meetings.'

'I will.' He thought about the suit he'd worn the previous night. And this made him think about Robin. Of all the times to have to jaunt off to London. But it was the opportunity of a lifetime.

'Remember,' his agent reminded him. 'Not a word of this to anyone. Consider it top secret until you've inked the deal, and the publishers have released the news. It's important that they make the deal known. Not you. And you've told me the gossip where you live is rife. So keep this to yourself for now.'

'I won't tell anyone,' he promised. Though he wished he could tell Robin, share the great news with her, and explain why he was heading to London. But he wouldn't. He would let her know he was leaving for a few days. Typical, just when he was hoping to ask her out.

'Congratulations, Oliver,' said his agent. 'I've a feeling this is going to be a success for you.'

'Thank you. I'll phone you later when I leave for Edinburgh.'

After the call, Oliver sorted out his morning business, put a message on his website that his shop was closed for a few days, but that he could be contacted via the website if necessary.

Then he went upstairs and packed a suitcase with everything he thought he'd need to look sharp for the meetings.

Bags packed, now all he had to do was make sure all the artwork was well presented in the portfolio. This took him the rest of the morning. The sunlight shone through the shop window as he sat the portfolio on the counter and checked each page of watercolour art. Seeing it again, in the bright daylight, a rush of excitement charged through him. This was the type of book he would've loved to read when he was a wee boy. Hopefully it would be a success.

It was early evening by the time he was ready to leave.

With everything packed in his car, including a satchel with his portfolio, sketch book, watercolour pad, travel tin of watercolour paints and brushes, pencils and pens, and wearing a light blue shirt, silk tie and dark trousers, he put a closed sign up on the window, secured the shop and drove off towards the loch — and Robin's cottage.

He planned to pop in and tell her personally that he was off to London and would be back soon.

But her cottage was in darkness in the warm early evening glow of an amber sky. The sun was still burnished bright, refusing to give way to the night.

Oliver sighed wearily. Where was she? He knew she'd intended going to the cove, but she'd be back by now. Unless she was at the castle, with Jonathan. His heart lurched at the thought of her being inveigled into Jonathan's schedule again.

But then he saw a couple of the crafting bee ladies heading into Etta's cottage. Her cottage was all lit up. A bee night must've been planned. Robin would be there.

He drove over and parked outside Etta's cottage and hurried up to the door. It was open, and he could hear the chatter and pleasant chaos, along with the tinkle of teacups and spoons. Yes, a bee night was definitely being held.

He knocked on the door, and Etta came scurrying along the hall, smiling when she saw him standing there.

'Oliver!' Etta exclaimed. 'What can I do for you? We're having a dressmaking night, so you'll have to avert your eyes.' She jokingly placed her hand up to shield him for peeping further into the hall. 'The girls are sewing sundresses for this hot weather. They're all running around in the half dolly duff.'

Oliver jolted and looked anywhere except into the cottage. 'Sorry, I didn't know—'

Etta cut–in. 'What was it you wanted?'

'I wanted to talk to Robin.'

'Oh, she's not dressed. We're just pinning her into a nice cotton fabric, a blue chambray, to make a pretty sundress,' Etta told him.

'Right, well, I won't interrupt,' he said, and started to back away, slightly embarrassed, hoping he didn't look like he was deliberately trying to have a sneaky peek. 'Enjoy your evening, Etta.' He waved without glancing back and headed to his car.

Etta sensed something was amiss and hurried after him. 'What's wrong, Oliver?' she said in a low and insistent whisper.

He paused and those concerned and disappointed green eyes of his looked right at her. 'Nothing, I'm just...off to London for two or three days. An impromptu business trip. My agent phoned with a deal I'd like to accept.'

'Is that the agent you told me about? The one that sorts out your artwork deals?'

'Yes, that's him. He's in Edinburgh. I'm driving there to meet him, and we're flying down to London first thing in the morning.' He gave no further details.

'Well, I hope it's a successful trip for you.' She smiled at him, but sensed there was something still amiss. 'What's wrong?' she whispered, so the other ladies didn't overhear them.

Oliver hesitated. He couldn't tell anyone, especially Etta.

She stepped closer. 'I know I'm the top gossipmonger around here, but I can keep a secret when I need to. You can trust me. What's wrong? Is it something to do with Robin?'

He nodded. 'I wanted to let her know where I'm going, and that I'll be back soon.'

Etta was wise enough to sense his underlying turmoil. 'It's an important deal, isn't it?'

'Yes,' he said.

'But you're worried about Robin...perhaps about her and Jonathan?'

He bit his lip and nodded again.

'I heard you did a lovely painting of her cottage, as a gift.'

'I did. I gave it to her last night.'

'She loves it.'

He smiled. 'I'm glad.'

'I'll explain to Robin that you're away to London. But if you're concerned about Jonathan making a play for her, don't worry. Jessy advised Gaven not to encourage Jonathan to wangle more time from Robin.'

'She did?'

'Yes, and Gaven told Jonathan this earlier today when he wanted to drop by her cottage so she could take him around the farming fields. So Jonathan's been told, by the laird, that Robin is busy, and he'll have to sort out his tours for himself,' said Etta.

Oliver's heart lifted.

'So you go and get them in London, Oliver. Grab any chances offered if you want them. We'll look after Robin. Jonathan and his wiles won't get by us.'

Oliver smiled. 'Jonathan versus the crafting bee ladies. I know who my money is on.'

Etta smiled at him. 'Now, have a safe trip. And send us pictures of the sights in London so we can live vicariously through you.'

'I will. I promise. Thanks, Etta.'

He got into his car, just as Aileen came out to see what was going on.

'What was Oliver wanting?' said Aileen.

'Nothing, just something to do with his art for Robin,' Etta lied.

Robin peeked out from behind the front door, clutching the makeshift dress that was pinned and barely covered her modesty. She saw Oliver's car drive off along the loch. 'Was Oliver wanting to speak to me?'

'Yes, he just wanted to let you know he's away for a few days to London and he'll see you when he gets back,' said Etta.

Robin watched the tail lights of Oliver's car disappear into the night, and her heart ached, wishing she'd seen him before he left, and yet delighted that he wanted to let her know he was leaving.

'Now, let's see that dress on you,' Etta said chirpily to Robin. 'Oh, yes, it needs a few tucks and darts in the bodice and the waistline, but the blue colour really suits you.'

Etta hurried Robin and Aileen inside the cottage to get on with their bee night.

'Would you put the kettle on again Aileen while I pin Robin's dress?' said Etta.

Several other members were running around helping each other make the easy pattern sundresses, and the sewing machine whirred in the living room as the seams were sewn.

Aileen was happy to make the tea and went through to the kitchen to fill the kettle and sort the cups.

'I've got an extra wee treat for us,' Etta called through to Aileen. 'There's a white chocolate cake filled with buttercream. It's Bradoch's latest chocolate cake recipe. I told him we enjoyed his other chocolate cake, so now we're forced to be his official cake testers.'

'It's a hard life, isn't it,' Aileen replied.

The ladies giggled.

Amid the laughter, chatter, dressmaking, tea and cake, gossip was exchanged, as always. But Etta kept her word to Oliver.

'Were you in swimming at the cove today?' Sylvia said to Robin as the chatter continued, along with eating the delicious white chocolate cake.

'I was,' said Robin. 'The water was quite warm. I hadn't been swimming in ages, and it was great having a day at the shore, splashing about in the sea. It's so beautiful at the cove.'

'You'd get a chance to enjoy it without Jonathan being there,' Etta remarked.

'Yes,' said Robin. 'I took my textile art with me, the seascape I'm working on and did a bit of embroidery. I've never stitched down the shore, but it was sooo relaxing.'

'I'll stitch anywhere,' said Sylvia. 'But you've put me in the notion of having a day at the cove.'

'I had lunch there,' Robin told them.

'At the restaurant?' said Aileen.

'No, a chip piece from one of the snack sellers. I saw Oliver having that when I was there with Jonathan,' Robin revealed.

Etta blinked. 'I didn't know Oliver was at the cove yesterday.'

'He was in swimming and trying, but not succeeding, to encourage Jonathan to go for a swim. But he wouldn't even go for a paddle. Jonathan said he doesn't do wild swimming.'

'Ach, my bahookie!' said Etta. 'He should've at least had a paddle in the sea.'

'I think Jonathan's a soor dook,' Sylvia reasoned. 'I don't think there's anything wild about him.'

'He's certainly not taking up more of your time, Robin,' Etta said firmly.

Robin didn't need encouraged. 'Nope.'

'Was Oliver wearing his trunks?' Sylvia said to Robin. And then giggled.

'He was,' Robin said, feeling herself blush.

'I bet he's got muscles,' said Sylvia.

'Oliver is deceivingly handsome,' Aileen remarked. 'And such a nice man.'

'He came striding out of the sea,' Robin told them, adding details that she then wished she hadn't embellished.

'Oh, I'm thinking you've got a wee fancy for Oliver,' said Etta.

Robin blushed, and sipped her tea.

'Oooh! We've got another romance brewing,' Aileen chirped.

Robin giggled and blushed even more. 'Stop it!'

The evening of dressmaking continued with members using Etta's sewing machine, and machines they'd brought with them.

'I love this blue chambray fabric,' said Robin. 'It's so soft and light. Perfect for a sundress.' It was an easy pattern without a zip in the back, ideal for whipping up in an evening for those skilled at sewing clothes.

Aileen and a couple of other members were experts at dressmaking and helped others, like Robin, machine their dresses.

The chambray fabric was from Aileen's quilt shop. She'd brought along a selection of a new range of summer cottons that could be used for making quilts, or for dressmaking and other crafts. Her shop in the main street was popular with the members, and Aileen added new fabrics on a regular basis to her stock. These were bought mainly by online customers, but provided an excellent source of fabric for the bee members. And members received a discount, further adding to the bargain buys. Off–cuts were sold as bundles suitable for crafts such as doll making, small quilted items like mug rugs, tea towels and cushions, as well as for patchwork quilts.

By the end of the evening, Robin's dress was almost ready to wear. 'I'll finish the hem in the morning,' she said, folding the dress and tucking it into her craft bag.

'Is that white chambray fabric?' Robin said to Aileen, seeing her packing away some of the fabric she'd brought with her to the bee night.

'It is,' said Aileen, letting Robin have a look at it. 'Three metres. Cotton.'

'I'll take it to make another dress for the summer,' Robin told Aileen. 'I love it.'

Aileen folded the fabric and gave it to Robin. 'And here's the dress pattern. Let me know if you need a hand to make it. Or pop into the quilt shop and I'll help you to fit it.'

With everyone agreeing that they'd had a great night, with many now having sundresses to wear or almost ready to wear, they bid Etta and each other goodnight and headed home.

Robin shrugged her bag on to her shoulder and walked around the loch to her cottage. It was such a lovely night, and she gazed up at the stars, shining bright. The air was scented with the surrounding greenery and flowers, and it felt so calming at the end of a busy but fun day.

The lantern glowed outside her cottage's front door, and she unlocked it and went inside.

In her bedroom, she hung the blue chambray dress up on the outside of the wardrobe so she could admire it. Then she went through to the living room and unpacked her craft bag, putting the folded white chambray beside her sewing machine along with the dress pattern.

The energetic events of the day were starting to catch up with her, and although she was tempted to hem the new dress to finish it, she knew she needed to get some sleep.

Tucked up in bed, she rewound her trip to the cove, swimming in the sea. She planned to have more days like that. Maybe one day Oliver would join her — as friends, and they could go swimming together. Her heart reacted just thinking about this, and she wondered if Etta was right. Was she attracted to Oliver? He could be a heartbreaker. And she didn't want to risk a broken heart.

But he was sooo good looking. In the back of her mind she'd always thought this, but as he'd never shown anything more than a friendly interest, she hadn't allowed herself to let these thoughts drift further.

She sighed heavily. Seeing Oliver at the cove recently had taken her aback. Oliver was hard to ignore with his tall, fit build, dark brown hair that was slightly ruffled and those gorgeous green eyes of his. And she loved that he was an artist. Something they had in common. He seemed to understand her work as a textile artist.

Wondering why he'd wanted to tell her he was leaving for London, and assure her he'd be back soon, she settled down to sleep. Things would look clearer in the morning.

But in her heart was a spark of hope of a summer romance.

CHAPTER EIGHT

Robin walked to Bradoch's bakery in the morning for fresh bread and rolls.

Bradoch's smile welcomed her in. 'You're early this morning, Robin. You've just missed Etta.'

'I think it's the bright summer weather. I want make the most of it.'

Bradoch bagged her bread and rolls. 'I hear you were swimming at the cove.'

'I was. I'm tempted to have a repeat performance today, but trying to talk sense into myself. I've work to do.'

'If your work can wait, you should head for the shore. I know I would.'

'I may just do that.'

'Do you know that Oliver is away on business to London?'

'Yes, he stopped by the crafting bee at Etta's cottage last night. I didn't get a chance to talk to him.'

Bradoch didn't push the conversation any further. 'Is there something else I can get for you?'

Robin eyed the cakes on display. 'I'll have one of your summer fruit and cream scones.'

Bradoch bagged the scone that was filled with fresh fruit including raspberries and brambles, and whipped cream.

Robin paid for her items, smiled at Bradoch and left as other customers came into the bakery.

Stepping outside into the morning sunlight, she glanced over at Oliver's art shop. Seeing it closed, her heart ached a little, but then she shrugged the feeling aside and walked back to her cottage to get on with her day.

The loch shone like smooth glass in the sunshine, and the scent of flowers perfumed the air. Her garden was looking lovely, she thought, and it made her decide to stay where she was, at the cottage, working and enjoying being out in her garden.

She popped the fruit and cream scone in the fridge, and cut two thick slices of fresh bread to make tasty buttered toast for her breakfast.

While the kettle boiled for tea, she checked her website for any online orders and was pleasantly surprised that she'd had several sales of substantial pieces of her textile art — like full paintings, original pieces that sold quite well. A trip to the post office would be needed, so after breakfast she packaged the orders up and took them along for posting.

She'd promoted these new pieces on her website as suitable for summer, with bright coloured floral designs, and summery turquoise blues, sunshine yellow and vibrant pinks.

On the way back, her phone rang. She paused at the edge of the loch to take the call from the knitwear company she modelled for.

'We're promoting our summer range in a fashion feature, and we'd like you to model several new pieces for us, Robin,' the management woman told her. 'Would you be available in a few days time? We're arranging a suitable location. You've been there before during the last photo shoot for the spring collection of jumpers and cardigans. The windswept coast north of where you are.'

'I know where you mean,' Robin confirmed.

'I'll email the details of the schedule. You have the right look for the new knitwear promotion. The usual fee applies, if that's okay with you, Robin.'

'Yes,' Robin agreed. The modelling money always came in handy, and she enjoyed the photo shoots. The location was a couple of hours drive from her cottage.

After the call, Robin went into her cottage and noticed a hand delivered letter had arrived. She opened the envelope and read it and smiled. It was an invitation to have lunch or dinner for two at the castle as Gaven's guests, in thanks to Robin for helping Jonathan. She surmised that Walter had dropped it off while she'd been at the post office.

Putting the invitation safely in her desk drawer, she sat outside in her back garden, embroidering a piece of textile art and relaxing until lunchtime.

Thoughts of Oliver kept drifting through her mind. She wondered how he was getting on in London. And what type of deal his agent had secured for him. Another commissioned collection for a home decor company? Something like that probably.

Stopping for lunch, she made a couple of tomato salad rolls and tea, and sat outside to eat them. Her back garden was looking lovely with more flowers flourishing in the warm weather.

She continued working on her art after lunch, finishing the seascape and making progress with a summer landscape.

In the afternoon she paused to have tea and the fruit and cream scone, and started work on something else — the two textile art pieces depicting her cottage. One daytime scene where she planned to emphasise the flowers in her garden, layering them in the foreground, then the loch and the cottage with the hills and summery blue sky in the background. The second one was the night version of the cottage that she'd started, using dark blue colours and textures like cotton and chiffon, embroidered with hints of silver and gold metallic thread for the stars and moonlight.

They required quite a bit of work, but working on both allowed her to make them into a beautiful set of two cottages by the loch in Scotland.

As the day wore on and became early evening, and the amber glow of golden hour swept across the cottage and the garden like a wash of watercolour, a warm sepia tint, she soaked in all the colours and the sense of it, the feeling of the day giving way to the evening. She took photos of it to use as references for the colours.

Dinner beckoned, but she didn't yet have an appetite, too fired up with creativity and enjoying her textile art work.

She went inside to her living room when the daylight finally faded, but continued fuelled only with cups of tea, until she had finished substantial parts of the two cottage scenes.

Finally, easing off the tension from her shoulders, she decided to make dinner. Something easy again. A bowl of lentil soup and a couple of slices of bread.

With the lamps in her living room casting a cosy glow, she worked after dinner until quite late at night, pausing for a cuppa or two, but happy to relax and enjoy an evening in doing what she loved.

When it was time for bed, she tidied everything away, turned the living room lights off and snuggled under the duvet.

She kept the bedroom window open to let in the fresh air. It was another warm night, with the view of the loch soothing her to sleep.

Oliver lay in bed in his hotel room in London, gazing out at the lights of the city. The meeting with the publishers had been a success, so much so, that they wanted to have a second meeting with him, a lunch meeting the following day.

The three–book deal was signed and sealed. Now he had to come up with the storylines for the other two books in the series. This was what they wanted to discuss with him — and his artwork. They loved the characters he'd created and the colours he'd used to depict them. The main editor wanted Oliver to include all the characters in the next two books. Oliver said he was happy to do this, and wanted to add other little creatures in the cottage garden as well. They loved this idea, and he liked the feeling of excitement that he was part of creating something special, books filled with artwork that were beautiful to look at and stories of the characters' adventures in the garden.

But his thoughts still dwelled on Robin, wondering what she was up to. He trusted that Etta and the crafting bee ladies wouldn't let Jonathan take advantage of her again, though that didn't stop him worrying about missing out on his chance to date Robin.

He considered phoning her, but he didn't have her personal number, only the one on her website. Apart from that, what he wanted to say to her, to ask her to have dinner with him, didn't merit being done in a phone call. He wanted to talk to her personally. So he planned to do this when he got back home from London.

His agent had explained that his work schedule for his art would have to change, giving time to the picture books. Oliver knew this, and agreed. The picture book dream had always been in the background, and now it had to become part of his work schedule. He couldn't wait to get back and start illustrating and painting the two new stories. The deal he'd signed was highly lucrative.

Everything was going to change. For the better. As an artist, he was about to take a huge step forwards towards further success. He had to make the most of it.

But where did that leave Robin?

When he thought about it, Robin was part of the reason he had the picture book deal. He'd liked her when he'd first met her, and planned to ask her out, but when he thought that she was dating a farmer, he'd held back, and felt disheartened. In the evenings, after working in his shop, he'd taken his mind off things by finishing the picture book he'd started and never completed. He worked on it for a few weeks, to finished artwork level, and wrote the story. He'd taken it upon himself to design a cover too.

When it was done, he didn't tell anyone and had put it aside, not sure what to do with it. The whole process of painting in the evenings, becoming lost in the picture book art, had soothed his heart.

Until fairly recently, the artwork had been tucked in a portfolio, but when talking to his agent about a deal for his paintings, he'd dared to mention that he had created a picture book. And now...here he was, in London, having inked a deal.

The meeting the next day was going to be hectic, as the publishers had decided to interview Oliver, and film a few minutes of it, for publicity purposes. And they'd seen that he had short videos of himself on his shop's website, demonstrating his painting techniques. So they wanted him to demonstrate the picture book artwork. He'd brought his travel watercolour kit with him, and a watercolour pad, so they intending filming this too. It was feasible that his two or three day trip to London would become four days, but it would be handy to do all the publicity shots while he was down there.

Gazing out his hotel window at the glittering lights of the city, he settled down to get some sleep. It was another early start in the morning.

Robin sat at her kitchen table and ate cereal and fruit for breakfast. The kitchen door was wide open, letting in the sunny morning.

An email had arrived telling her the details for the knitwear modelling, and as she'd done this several times before, she was happy with the schedule. They wanted her to wear her long, strawberry blonde hair down for most of the pictures, with a few shots with it pinned up in a wispy chignon. Again, this is what had worked well before. They had hair and makeup staff for the shoot, but Robin always arrived with her hair freshly washed and dried smooth. All the clothes would be supplied. Pictures of the summer lace weight cardigans, short sleeve jumpers and pretty knitted tops were attached to the message, and she loved the bright pastel colours of the new range.

After breakfast, she started work on her textile designs, and finished the two cottage scenes — the daylight version and the night scene. They looked so pretty that she decided to keep them for herself rather than sell them, but she planned to create variations of the cottages and put them up for sale on her website. She kept spare frames and mounting boards in her cupboard, and worked on framing her two pieces of textile art. The frames were beige with creamy white borders and looked great with the cottage scenes. She hung them beside Oliver's watercolour painting of her cottage. They looked wonderful on her wall.

By the afternoon she'd packed up a few online orders for customers and taken them to the post office.

In the main street, she met Etta, and saw a couple of photos Oliver had sent her, as promised, of London.

'He should be home soon,' said Etta. 'Has he contacted you?'

'No, but he doesn't have my personal number,' Robin told her.

'Do you want me to give him your number?' Etta offered.

'No, no, it's okay.'

'Well, he seems to be getting on fine whatever he's up to.'

Robin told her about the knitwear modelling.

'Oooh! Exciting. I'm sure you'll look lovely,' said Etta.

'I'm looking forward to it. I love wearing the gorgeous knitwear, and I always have a fun time during the photo shoots. The weather is going to be great, so the pictures should be ideal for the summer promotion.' Robin scrolled through her phone and showed Etta the items she'd be wearing.

'I love the light blue yarn they've used to knit the cardigan.'

'Apparently, it's a new yarn. I love the colour too. It reminds me of the blue chambray dress. I've still the hem to finish, but I intend stitching that by hand later. I'm going to wear the dress to the modelling assignment along with a lightweight white cardigan.'

'That's sounds perfect.'

They were still chatting about knitting and yarn when Sylvia came out of Bradoch's bakery with two strawberry tarts for her afternoon tea with her aunt at the sweet shop.

'Bradoch's a rascal,' Sylvia said jokingly. 'I went in there to give him the jelly sweets he'd ordered, and there he was tempting me with strawberry tarts.' She shrugged. 'But they'll be tasty for our afternoon tea. We've been busy making tablet and toffee sweets today. Lunch was a hurried sandwich, so I'm ready for a cuppa and a treat.'

'I'll walk back with you to the sweet shop,' said Etta. 'I like your tablet, so I'll have a bar of that and a bag of your mixed favourites.'

Waving to each other, Robin headed back home while Etta went with Sylvia to the sweet shop.

Walking along the side of the loch, the sunlight sparkled on the surface, and more flowers had sprung up around part of the edges. The cornflowers wafted in the warm breeze, and she took close–up photos of the blue petals and the deep blue hue in the heart of them. Pink roses were blooming along with blue daisies, and bees were buzzing, attracted to the flowers. Butterflies fluttered around and the fragrance from the flowers felt like nature's aromatherapy. She even glimpsed dragonflies flitting over the loch.

And she thought about Oliver. The photos he'd sent Etta showed a busy street in London during the day, and a picture overlooking the city from the window of his hotel at night. Her heart reacted just thinking about him.

The jars of sweets in the window of the sweet shop glistened with sugar crystals in the sun. Sylvia lifted one of the jars down and measured out a portion into a paper bag for Etta.

The shop with its quaint canopy was opposite Oliver's art shop. Sylvia helped her Aunt Muira make and sell a popular selection of confectionery, specialising in vintage, traditional and all sorts of sweets. Sylvia had only been there since Christmas when she came to work in her aunt's pretty little sweet shop.

'Do you want a couple of orange jellies and barley sugar?' Sylvia offered her.

'Yes, and one or two chocolates,' said Etta.

Sylvia lifted other jars down, scooped up a varied selection, added them to the bag and then handed it to Etta. 'That should keep you going.'

Etta paid for her sweeties, and then called through to Sylvia's aunt working in the kitchen at the back of the shop. 'Something smells delicious, Muira.'

Muira popped her head round the kitchen door. 'I'm making an order of butterscotch for Gaven. They've added vanilla ice cream with butterscotch sauce to their dinner menu, and the head chef put pieces of our butterscotch with it. They had some of it leftover from a previous batch we made for them. Anyway, now the guests expect a piece of butterscotch with their ice cream, so Gaven phoned to ask if we'd make a rush order for him.'

'I like butterscotch with vanilla ice cream,' said Etta. 'You've put me in the notion now.'

Sylvia smiled. 'There's a couple of squares in your sweetie selection.'

'Oh, great. I've vanilla ice cream in my freezer, so I know what I'm having with my dinner tonight.'

Muira laughed. 'Snap. We've put ourselves in the notion of it, so we're picking up vanilla ice cream from the wee shop after we close tonight.'

Etta smiled, went to leave and then paused to show them Oliver's photos.

'Oliver sent these from London.' Etta held up her phone to show them.

'It's ages since I was there,' said Muira. 'Do we know what he's up to yet? Has he sold paintings to one of the companies down there?'

'He hasn't said yet,' Etta told Muira. 'I think he wants it all settled before he tells us, but it's bound to do with his beautiful paintings. His agent has probably got him a great deal for them.'

'I often admire the paintings on display in the window of his shop,' said Muira. 'And we're excited that our sweet shop is included in his new collection for that home decor company.'

'Maybe it's a deal like that he's got again,' Sylvia suggested.

The women nodded, and then with a cheery wave, Etta left the shop taking her bag of sweets with her. Unable to resist having one to keep her going while she walked back to her cottage, she popped a chocolate in her mouth and enjoyed it along with the warmth of the sunny day.

By the evening, Robin finished up her textile art, tidied everything away, and then got ready for bed. Setting her alarm, she went to bed to get a decent night's sleep, and was looking forward to her modelling trip.

CHAPTER NINE

Sunlight shone through the early morning blue sky as Robin packed an overnight bag, and a duffel bag with accessories just in case she needed them for the photo shoot.

She'd been up at first light, showered, washed and dried her hair, and put on her new blue chambray dress that she'd hemmed by hand.

The dew glistened on the grass and flowers in her garden as she stepped out into the sunny morning.

She put her bags, a denim jacket and the white cardigan in the back of her car, secured the cottage and then drove off along the loch, heading for the road that wound past Gaven's castle and into the countryside.

The drive to the location of the photo shoot wasn't too far, and the summer day made it all the more pleasant.

Three other models were taking part in modelling the knitwear, and she recognised them as she drove up and parked outside the trailer that was set up for the wardrobe and hair and makeup purposes.

It felt like meeting up with friends she hadn't seen in a while, including the knitwear company's head of features and publicity. Robin always got along well with her.

Robin was welcomed into the busy hub, seated in front of the hair and makeup unit alongside the other models, given a cup of tea, and while the stylists created the look they needed, chatter and gossip was exchanged as they all caught up with each other's news.

In the late afternoon, Oliver and his agent flew back to Edinburgh after their successful trip to London.

Oliver had dinner in Edinburgh with his agent to discuss their plans for the new picture books, and then he drove home to the village.

After the hustle and bustle of the previous few days, he was glad to be back to the calm of the countryside and the loch.

It had been agreed that his publishers would release the news about his new picture book the following day, and get the ball rolling on the publicity, so Oliver was now able to tell Robin and others at the village about where he'd been and what he'd been up to.

Robin was on his mind, as always, and he planned to drop by her cottage on the way to his shop, to let her know he was back — and for her to be the first one he told about his book deal.

The winding road through the countryside led past the castle, and one of the turrets was lit up against the dark sky. It wasn't that late, but there was a richness to the night, as if the summer was adding warmth to the evening and extending it with the feeling of a hot summer season.

The road led on through the trees and down to the loch that glistened like dark glass in the evening's glow. He felt himself relax just looking at it. And then he glanced towards Robin's cottage, expecting the lights to be shining in the windows, unless she was at one of the other cottages for a crafting night.

As he drove nearer, he saw that Robin's cottage was in darkness. Not even a glow from the wall lantern. There was a sense that she'd turned everything off and hadn't been there all day, and wasn't due to be there that evening.

He frowned, wondering where she was. Wondering too if he was overtired from his trip and reading things wrong.

Pulling up, he got out of his car and walked up to the door, knocked and waited for a response. Nothing. He sighed wearily. He was right. Robin wasn't in.

The lights were on in Etta's cottage on the other side of the loch, so he drove there, parked outside and knocked on the front door. Unlike other evenings when a crafting bee was being held there, the door was closed and no lively chatter and activity sounded from inside.

Etta came to the door and looked surprised when she saw Oliver standing there.

'Oh, you're home!' She sounded pleased to see him. 'I didn't know you were back.'

'I've just arrived.' He glanced across at Robin's cottage. 'Do you know where Robin is?'

'She's away doing her knitwear modelling,' Etta explained.

'Ah, I didn't know she was doing that.'

'Yes, she left this morning and was due to come back this evening, but she phoned to tell me that she's staying overnight. Sometimes she has to do that. The photo shoot went so well that the knitwear company are extending it to another day. Robin asked me to keep an eye on her cottage.'

Oliver looked a bit lost. His own mistake. He hadn't even considered that Robin would be away just as he got back.

'Do you want to come in for a cup of tea—'

'No, but thanks. I'm worn from travelling and everything.'

He didn't volunteer any details of what he'd been up to, so Etta didn't ask him. He wanted Robin to be the first to know, but maybe that plan was due to go awry.

'Yes, of course,' she said. 'I got the photos you sent. I showed them to a few of the ladies and we were hoping you were getting on okay.'

'I did. And tomorrow I'm going to tell everyone what I was doing in London.'

Etta smiled. 'Well, it's nice to have you back, and I'll look forward to hearing your news.'

'Goodnight, Etta.' He walked back to his car.

She smiled again and then went back inside her cottage.

Oliver drove to his shop, feeling relieved to unlock the front door and step inside. The shop was calm, quiet and he felt he was back where he belonged after his hectic trip.

He took his suitcase and bag upstairs, unpacked his things and got ready for bed.

Tiredness swept over him as his head hit the pillow, and he slept sound until the morning.

Milk. Oliver peered in the fridge. He wanted a cup of tea to get his morning started, but he'd cleared it of milk and other items.

The morning was bright and breezy, and he walked to the wee shop for milk and fresh groceries, and then popped into Bradoch's bakery for rolls and a loaf.

Bradoch was serving a customer, but smiled when he saw Oliver walk in.

The customer left with a bag of cakes and sticky iced buns, and Bradoch welcomed Oliver.

'How was your trip to London?' Bradoch said, bagging up rolls and a loaf for Oliver.

'It was worthwhile, but I'm glad to be home.'

'I'm not much of a traveller myself,' Bradoch confessed. 'I've been to a few places, but I'm more of a homebody.'

Oliver nodded. 'So am I.' He eyed the savoury cheese and onion pastries. 'I'll have one of your pastries and a mashed potato puff pastry.'

Bradoch added these to Oliver's order.

Oliver glanced at him. 'Okay, so what else are you going to tempt me with this morning?'

Bradoch gestured to the display cabinet. 'An iced bun with whipped cream and bramble jam.'

'I'll have one.'

Bradoch smiled, popped it in a bag, and handed Oliver his order as he paid for it.

'Is your trip still top secret?' Bradoch said to him as Oliver went to leave.

Oliver shook his head. 'I'm hoping to tell Robin first, but she's away doing her knitwear modelling.'

'She won't be away for long though. Then we'll all find out what you were up to.'

Oliver smiled and nodded. 'Yes, see you later.' He left as another two customers came in.

Walking across to his shop he started to think about ideas for the new picture books, feeling excited about sketching roughs and doing light washes of watercolour to plan the look of the second book.

But first he made himself breakfast and a pot of tea, tackled the online orders, replied to messages, cleared the decks of the shop work, and then set himself up to make a start on the new picture book. He'd agreed to send the roughs to the publisher.

He became lost in his work, enjoying creating new scenes for the second picture book.

Checking the publisher's website, his heart jolted. They'd put the news of his deal on their front page, along with the interview. No one locally would know to search for this, so he was sure that he'd still be able to tell them first. But he hadn't reckoned on the news hitting other sites, and by the late afternoon the gossip had started.

Fyn was the first to come bounding across from his flower shop.

'I'm buying your big watercolour painting, as an investment, before you get too famous and up your prices,' Fyn joked with him.

Oliver sighed. 'You've heard the news.'

'Everybody has heard the news. Congratulations. It's well–deserved. That was a great interview with the publisher. And were you really painting live while they filmed you?'

'I was.'

'That was impressive. I wish I could paint like that. I wish I could paint even a wee bit, but I'll stick to working with my flowers and leave the artwork to you.'

Bradoch came barging in — with a cake. He'd stuck a candle on the top.

'Etta's holding the fort at my bakery,' Bradoch said, grinning cheerily. He sparked a lighter and lit the candle.

Oliver laughed.

'Come on!' Bradoch urged him. 'You've got something great to celebrate.'

Fyn encouraged him too. 'Make a wish, though I think you've probably had it come true already with your book deal.'

Oliver took a deep breath and blew out the candle — and made a wish. He did have his dream come true in having his picture book accepted for publication, but there was something else he longed for.

Bradoch put the Victoria sponge cake, sandwiched with strawberry jam and cream, down on the counter. 'I have to run back to deal with my customers, but Gaven's talking about throwing a party for you at the castle.'

Leaving his words hanging temptingly in the air, Bradoch hurried out and ran back across the road to his bakery.

Fyn and Oliver were left standing smiling, though Oliver was taken aback.

'I didn't expect a party — at the castle,' said Oliver.

'We always celebrate a local person's success. Gaven threw a party for me when I opened my flower shop.'

'Okay, then. A party it is.'

'You've no excuses now. You'll have to ask Robin to go as your date to the party.'

'She's away modelling knitwear.'

'Ach, she'll be back soon. Don't fret.'

Oliver's phone started ringing, and his website lit up with messages.

'I'll let you get on. Well done again, Oliver. We're all proud of you. And I am buying that painting!'

Laughing and waving, Fyn ran back to his flower shop as Oliver fielded the incoming calls. One was from a Scottish daily newspaper wanting a direct quote from him. They were running the story via the press release on the publisher's website. It would hit the headlines in the next day's edition of the paper.

Another call was from his agent. 'My phone's on fire.'

'So is mine. I've had one of the daily papers asking me for a quote.'

'What did you tell them?'

'I said I'm working on the second picture book in the series.'

'Are you?' his agent sounded surprised.

'Yes, I was sketching and trying light washes with my watercolours.'

'That's great.'

'They asked about me opening a shop here and living above the shop, so I told them what it's like. And they wanted me to elaborate on the artist's break I took last year at one of the cabins at Gaven's castle. I gave them details about enjoying a painting holiday, and fell in love with the area so I moved here. They seemed to like that I was painting at a castle cabin in the Scottish Highlands near a loch. I think that's the angle they're going for.'

'People love a success story, especially if it's somewhere in the wilds of Scotland where it looks beautiful and romantic.'

'They've asked if I can email a photo of myself painting at the loch — and one with the castle in the background. I'll need to phone Gaven and tell him, though I've heard he's planning a party for me at the castle to celebrate the news. He takes it upon himself to do this for anyone in the local community that does well, opens a new shop, things like that.'

'I think Gaven will be over the moon to hear that his castle will get even more of a mention in the press. I saw that you spoke about taking a break at the castle in the interview on the publisher's news.'

Oliver sighed. 'Yes, but I didn't expect my book deal news to spark so fast.'

'Take the interest while it's going. It'll spark for one or two days, then it'll quieten down and you can get on with painting the new book,' his agent assured him.

'Okay, I'm going to phone Gaven.'

'Keep me up to date. Phone if you need my help.'

'Cheers,' said Oliver, and then phoned Gaven at the castle.

'Congratulations,' Gaven said before Oliver had a chance to tell him what the press wanted.

Oliver explained the details.

'I'll drive down and pick you up,' said Gaven. 'And if you want, I'll take photos of you painting at the loch.'

'That would be helpful. I'll grab my paint stuff.'

'I'll be down at the shop in about ten minutes.'

After the phone call, Oliver hurried up to gather the items he used when painting outdoors. He had a paint box with his favourite colours, brushes, a bottle of water and small containers for the water. The paints, brushes, pencils and other items were the same as the ones he used in his studio. He often painted outdoors, so he was used to packing things up into a couple of bags — including a folding easel, a board and watercolour paper that he taped to the board.

He'd already showered and wore a clean, light blue shirt and dark grey cords, so he figured he wouldn't need to change his clothes. He looked tidy and presentable for the photos.

Gaven drove up and parked outside the art shop.

Oliver hurried out, locking the shop, and put his bags in the back of Gaven's car.

'We'll take the photos at the loch and then head up to the castle,' said Gaven.

'Great.' Oliver looked out the window as they drove off to the nearby loch. The sun was streaming through the windows and the sky was a cloudless blue.

There were at the loch in minutes. Gaven pulled up near the edge and they both got out.

Gaven shielded his eyes from the sunlight. He'd brought his camera with him. 'If you set your paints up over there, I should be able to get a picture of you beside the loch without the glare of the direct sun.'

Oliver grabbed his equipment from the car and set it up. 'I brought a folding stool but I often stand when I'm painting and thought I'd do that. And I've got one of the rough watercolours I was working on for the new book.'

Gaven looked through the lens. He took all the pictures of the castle and estate for his website, so he was used to taking photos of the area. 'Stand beside the easel and hold one of the brushes as if you're painting.'

Oliver did as Gaven suggested.

Gaven took a few pictures and then they moved position to make sure they had other photos to select from.

Robin's cottage happened to be caught in the background, along with bees, butterflies and dragonflies fluttering through the flowers and over the loch. The sunlight glinted off the water, and these were the pictures they both liked when checking through them.

'These look great,' said Gaven.

Oliver agreed. 'You've captured everything the newspaper said they were looking for.' He loved that Robin's cottage was included behind him near the loch.

'I'll give you a copy of all of them,' Gaven told him.

Oliver packed his artwork up, and they drove the short distance to the castle and parked outside one of the self–catering log cabins.

'This is the one I had when I was here,' Oliver said, smiling.

'It's vacant today, but a designer is booking in tomorrow. Stand outside and I'll take a few shots.'

Oliver was happy to do this. 'I never took any photos of the cabin so these will be nice to have anyway.'

Gaven took several pictures. The cabin was situated within the trees, offering a lovely location and privacy for guests wanting to relax and work on their art, writing or other crafts.

Jonathan's cabin was on the other side of the trees, and there were no prying eyes from him or any of the other guests.

'Do you want a few pictures inside the cabin?' Gaven offered. 'Just for yourself, if you didn't take any when you were here.'

'Yes, thanks.'

Gaven fetched a set of keys from the car and opened the front door.

Oliver stepped inside and smiled, remembering how much he'd enjoyed painting there. The large window let in plenty of light, and there was an easel and work desk as part of the furniture.

Gaven took photos of Oliver standing near the easel with the light pouring in.

Then they went back out to the car and stood talking for a few minutes in the sunshine.

'That didn't take long,' said Gaven. 'It'll let you get the photos off to the newspaper this morning.'

'My agent says things will be hectic for a couple of days and then quieten down again.'

'Yes, so grab the opportunities while they're available,' Gaven advised him.

'I will.'

'We'll organise a party night at the castle soon,' Gaven promised. 'A cheery get together — a buffet and dancing.'

'I really appreciate it. I didn't expect a party.'

'Jessy said that Robin is away modelling knitwear,' said Gaven. 'She's missing all the news.'

'I know. I wanted to tell her myself, but...' he shrugged.

'She'll catch up on all the news when she gets back.'

As they went to get into the car, Jessy came hurrying towards them. 'Walter said you were here. I've got some news — about Jonathan.'

Gaven frowned. 'What about him?'

'He's booked out of his cabin, cut his artist's holiday short,' Jessy explained. 'I asked him why he was leaving and he said it was because he wasn't feeling the right artistic vibe here.' She glanced at Oliver. 'But we're thinking it's because his nose is out of joint hearing about Oliver's book deal.' She looked again at Oliver, as if to reassure him. 'So, Jonathan's gone.'

Gaven looked relieved. 'Oh well, maybe he'll find the vibe he's looking for somewhere else.' He smiled at Jessy.

'But,' Jessy added, 'we've been getting calls from people wanting to book an artistic break at the cabins.' She smiled at Oliver. 'Your great news is stirring up a lot of interest in the castle and the village.'

'I'm driving Oliver to his shop and then I'll be back to help with the bookings and lunch guests,' Gaven said to Jessy.

Jessy nodded and smiled at Gaven and Oliver, and then hurried away to the castle.

Gaven drove them along the edge of the loch and then on to the main street. They chatted about the party, making plans.

He parked outside the art shop.

Oliver grabbed his art equipment from the back of the car. 'Thanks again for your help.'

'Good luck with your pictures for the newspaper, Oliver.' Waving, Gaven drove off and headed back to the castle.

CHAPTER TEN

A twilight amber and lilac sky arched over the countryside as Robin drove home after another successful day's modelling. It had been fun wearing the beautiful knitwear fashions, and meeting and chatting with the other models and knitwear company staff. The weather had been gorgeous, out in the Scottish countryside, the wilds of the Highlands. They'd stayed at a lovely mansion hotel.

Despite enjoying the short trip away, she was looking forward to being back home, putting her feet up, relaxing in the comfort of her cottage and getting on with her textile art. She rarely had a day when she didn't paint or stitch something, and her fingers were itching to sit down with her fabric and embroidery thread again. Being away certainly made her realise how fortunate she was to make a living out of her textile art. The money she earned from the modelling was a handy boost, but she made a fairly steady and comfortable amount from her own work.

The castle's turret peering through the trees was the landmark that reassured her she was nearly at the loch, nearly home. For hundreds of years the castle itself had stood there, strong and steady. She liked the feeling of reliability and permanence it exuded, and a sense that it protected the village, and strengthened the community. Travelling further afield was fine and she enjoyed trips away, but at heart she was a homebody.

A glimpse of the loch shimmering through the trees made her heart lift. She was almost home.

Oliver put his watercolour pad and watercolour pencils in a satchel, hooked it up on to his shoulder and stepped out of his shop into the twilight lit main street. He'd rolled up the sleeves of his light blue shirt, and felt the warmth of the evening air against his bare arms. It felt like the heart of the summer, one of those evenings when the summer is at its height, and yet it was early in the season. There would be a lot of other nights like this to look forward to.

He'd had a light dinner — the mashed potato puff pastry from the bakery, and had decided to unwind after the hectic day of fielding phone calls from people wanting to talk to him about his book deal, and answering emails on the same topic. The newspaper was happy with the photos he'd sent them, and the story was due out in their paper the following morning. A news piece that was, according to his agent, going to spark even more interest in his picture books. But Oliver planned to deal with that in the morning.

Now, he just wanted to breathe a little, and as the loch was nearby, and like one of the fictional locations in his next book, he decided to go there while there was still enough light in the day to draw a few sketches and enjoy the early evening air.

Walking towards the loch, everything looked so calm, and he sat down where he'd had his photos taken earlier in the day.

Digging the watercolour pad and pencils from his satchel, he began sketching the flowers around the edge of the loch, and smiled when he saw a couple of dragonflies with their ethereal wings skimming over the surface of the water and whizzing through the flowers. One of the dragonflies stopped and settled on a thistle, with its wings open, giving Oliver a perfect view of its beautiful structure and azure blue colours.

Lights shone from the cottages dotted around the area, though Robin's was steeped in darkness. He hadn't dared get his hopes up that she'd be home this evening. But a pang of longing to see her and disappointment shot through him. He pushed the thoughts aside and continued sketching, using the watercolour pencils, dry on the paper, but it was enough to indicate the colours for reference when he came to paint the scenes.

He had the whole area to himself and gazed up at the vast sky casting an amber glow over everything. Soon, the sky would be a magnificent inky blue, but he planned to include the golden amber ambiance in his artwork and storyline for the next book. A night–time adventure for his little creature characters — bees, wasps, butterflies, dragonflies, moths, greenflies, ladybirds, and others, was the main theme of the second book in the series.

From the main street, a farm vehicle drove along the loch, heading home to one of the farms in the nearby countryside. Oliver was taken aback when the driver smiled at him and gave him a wave and thumbs up, indicating that he'd heard the latest news and was happy for him.

Oliver smiled and waved back, but as he was distracted, he didn't notice the car drive along the other side of the loch and stop outside Etta's cottage.

Robin carried a bag of yarn — skeins of the pretty light blue yarn used to make the cardigan from the new knitwear collection. Etta had admired the yarn when Robin showed her pictures of what she was going to be wearing for the photo shoot.

Etta opened the door. 'Oh, I'm glad you're home. Come on in.'

'I'll come in for a minute.' Robin stepped into the hall wearing her blue chambray dress and white cardigan. She handed Etta the bag of yarn.

Etta blinked and peered inside.

'It's samples of the new yarn,' said Robin. 'You said you liked the colour. The company always have freebie samples to give during a photo shoot, so I thought you'd like this. There's enough to knit a cardigan or a jumper.'

'This is so thoughtful of you, Robin. I love this blue colour.' She felt the texture of the yarn. 'It feels so soft. It'll be a treat to knit with.'

'I mentioned to them that you're an expert knitter, and eh...you can say no, but would you like to be added to their contact list of knitters that receive samples of new yarns to give their opinion on the quality, the colour, that sort of thing.'

'Me? Yes, I'd love to try out their yarn for them.' Etta sounded delighted, and gave Robin a hug. 'You're a wee gem, Robin.'

Robin was pleased that Etta liked the yarn and wanted to be part of the knitting company's contacts.

'Do you want to sit down for a cuppa?' Etta offered.

Robin sighed. 'I think if I sit down I'll not get back up. I'm happily tired, and I should get back to my cottage.'

Etta understood, but as Robin walked away, she called to her. 'Oliver is back from London. He was looking for you.'

Robin glanced back. 'Was he?' Her heart soared. She'd been thinking about him so much.

'Yes, he just missed you the morning you left.' Etta giggled. 'The pair of you seem to keep missing each other.'

'Do you know what he wanted?' said Robin.

Etta almost told her about Oliver's news, but buttoned her lips. Clearly, Robin hadn't heard about the book deal. The gossipmonger in her wanted to tell, but she fought the urge, and won. There was still a chance that Oliver could tell Robin.

'I don't know,' Etta lied, smiling tightly.

Robin looked thoughtful. 'Maybe I'll drop by his shop before I go home. It's not that late.'

'You should,' Etta encouraged her. 'He'll probably be working on his new...paintings, and other things, whatever he's painting.' She waffled and her words trailed off, covered by another encouraging smile.

Robin didn't pick up on Etta's suspicious attitude. All she was thinking about was she had a good reason now to go to Oliver's shop. After all, he'd been looking for her.

Etta waved Robin off, and then closed her cottage door, excited to try a few rows of the new yarn.

Spotlights illuminated the window display of the art shop, but no other lights shone from inside.

Robin knocked on the door and waited. And knocked again. And waited.

Nothing.

She stepped back and looked up at the windows where he lived above the shop. Everything was in darkness, indicating that Oliver wasn't at home.

Sighing wearily, she got into her car and drove off, heading to her cottage beside the loch.

Oliver was sketching the wings of a dragonfly when car headlights shone in the near distance. The glare from the lights stopped him from identifying the car, but as they were coming from the main street direction, he didn't think for a moment that it was Robin.

She saw the figure of a man lit up in the beam of the headlights. She blinked and muttered to herself. 'Oliver?'

As she drove nearer, she saw the figure start to walk away up the hill carrying a satchel on his shoulder. Yes, she thought, it was Oliver. What was he doing, and where was he going?

Oliver trudged up the hillside, determined to capture the glow of the evening from the top of the hill before calling it a night. The twilight was fading fast, giving way to the depth of the evening. The air was still warm, but soon there wouldn't be enough light to continue sketching. But if he was quick, he'd see the loch shimmering in the last of the gloaming.

Robin parked her car at the bottom of the hill near her cottage, and got out as the tall silhouette of Oliver disappeared from view.

'Oliver!' Robin shouted, hoping he'd hear her. 'Oliver!'

He stopped, hearing someone call his name. And not just anyone. It was Robin.

Hurrying to where he could see her, he shouted back. 'Robin. Wait.'

She waited, watching him walk back down the hillside.

His smile melted her heart.

He fought the urge to wrap her in his arms and hug the breath from her. Instead, he welcomed her home.

'I'm so glad you're home.'

'So am I.'

'Did you have a good trip?' he said.

'I did. I had a really nice time and the modelling shoot went well. They extended it and I stayed overnight in a mansion hotel. I could've stayed overnight again, but I decided to drive home tonight.'

'You must be tired.'

'Yes, sort of.' But she was feeling a burst of energy seeing Oliver when she hadn't expected him.

She glanced at his satchel and at the darkening sky. 'What are you doing?'

'Painting. Well, sketching with watercolour pencils to be precise.'

'Right.'

'I know it's dark, but it was a golden twilight when I started. The light faded fast.'

'Are you painting a night scene?'

'I am, planning it anyway, getting the feeling, the atmosphere sketched and ideas for the colours.' He glanced at the loch. 'I'm including the loch and some of the creatures in the flowers around it.'

'I've seen dragonflies lately,' she told him.

'Yes, I saw them.' He popped open his satchel, took out his watercolour pad and showed her the rough drawings.'

'You've captured the dragonfly's wings perfectly.' She studied the creature. 'It looks like it has a sort of personality, like a little character.'

Robin. Didn't. Know. The realisation struck him. He'd been so happy to see her, he'd pushed his news aside.

'Are you okay?' she said, seeing the look on his face.

'Yes.' He was more than okay. 'There's something I want to tell you.'

'Is it about your trip to London?'

He nodded and smiled...and took a deep breath...

'I've been offered a three–book deal for picture books. I've illustrated the first one in watercolours. I've written the story too. My agent secured the deal with a publisher in London. I couldn't tell anyone until the deal was signed.'

'Wow!' She was truly taken aback. 'I thought maybe it was your paintings, another home decor deal. I didn't know you illustrated picture books.'

'It's my first. I've been working on it for a long time. It was half finished, and I'd tucked it away for ages. Then fairly recently, I dug it out and worked on finishing it in the evenings after I'd closed the shop for the day.'

Robin was still taking in the news. 'Is this going to change everything for you? I mean, will you keep the shop?'

'Oh, yes. Things are a bit hectic at the moment.' He explained about the press coverage and publicity. 'My agent says it'll calm down soon, and I'll be able to work on the new books, while continuing my art shop business.'

'You're going to be extra busy.' Her heart was delighted for him, and yet the realisation started to sink in. They'd barely had any time together, and now Oliver was going to be busy with the picture books.

Oliver sensed from the look on Robin's face that she'd started to wonder if there would be any time left in his busy schedule. Don't hesitate, he told himself, and then heeded the warning.

'Would you like to have dinner with me?' Oliver said outright.

Robin blinked, taken aback.

'At the castle. And be my...sort of a date...for the party at the castle. Gaven's throwing a party for me to celebrate the news of the book deal.'

Robin felt a smile rise up. 'Sort of a date?'

Oliver wondered if he'd overstepped the mark. 'To accompany me to the party. There's going to be a buffet and dancing.' He hoped he wasn't waffling. Then bit his lips. He was definitely waffling. 'We could go together, to the party. You and me, and—'

'Yes,' she said, smiling at him, hearing him waffle.

Oliver blinked. 'Yes, you'll go with me to the party?'

'Yes.'

'Okay. That's wonderful. Gaven hasn't set a date yet, but it'll be in the next few nights. He took photos of me painting at the loch today for a newspaper. The story is coming out tomorrow. Your cottage is in the background.'

'My cottage?'

'It wasn't intentional. It was the angle of the picture. But just so you know if you see the paper and recognise your cottage, unless they crop it out, but I don't think they can. It's right behind me in the photo.'

'That's funny, my cottage will be in the newspaper.'

He suddenly heard voices approaching nearby, and realised it was neighbours heading to their cottages. Nope, he thought. No one and nothing was going to interrupt his conversation with Robin.

Grabbing her hand he encouraged her to run up the hill with him. 'Come on, Robin. Run.'

Laughing, trying not to stumble in the grass and heather covered hill, she ran holding tight to Oliver's hand, neither of them stopping until they were at the top. They had it all to themselves.

'It's bad when we have to resort to running away, to the top of the hills, to get five minutes alone time,' she said, smiling.

Oliver kept hold of her hand and she made no motion to let go of his.

Standing holding hands, gazing at the view of the loch below on one side of the hill, and the panorama of lights twinkling from cottages and farmhouses in the fields surrounding them, they sighed in unison.

'I've been wanting to ask you to have dinner with me for a while now,' he confessed.

'Why didn't you?'

He shrugged his broad shoulders. 'I thought you were dating one of the farmers. Fyn's brother, Gare.'

'I don't even know Fyn's brother.'

'No, it was crossed wires, gossip gone awry, but I believed it at the time and didn't want to cause trouble for you if you already had a boyfriend.'

'I've been so busy with my work, moving here, everything. I haven't had a boyfriend in ages, and nothing ever to write home about.'

He turned to face her. 'I thought maybe we could take things slowly. I heard that you didn't want to get romantically involved this summer, that you wanted to concentrate on your textile art and enjoy a carefree summertime.'

'That's true.' But then Oliver started to overturn her well–meaning plans. 'But slowly sounds sensible, and we are, if nothing else, sensible sorts.'

Oliver nodded, though he completely disagreed that he was sensible at all, especially when it came to his feelings for Robin.

'Will you have to go away again soon, to London?'

'No, but the publisher is pushing the first picture book through their process and planning to release it at Christmastime.'

'That's quick, though I don't know the whole publishing process, just what I've read.'

'It is fast, and when it comes out, I will have to do the rounds to publicise it, including a trip or two to London.'

'It'll be nice at Christmastime.'

'You've been?'

'Once, at Christmas years ago. All the lights, the decorations, the buzz of the city. It was great.'

'Maybe you'd enjoy another trip. This time with me.'

'You'd include me?'

He shrugged, trying to sound casual. 'If you'd like to come with me.'

'Yes, I'd like that.'

His heart soared, feeling that she liked him enough to plan to be with him at Christmastime.

'I've agreed with the knitwear company to do another modelling assignment for them in the autumn,' she told him. 'If you're not too busy, maybe you'd like to come along. You could bring your artwork.'

'I'd love to,' he said eagerly.

She looked around at the view. 'I never realised you can see the castle turrets from here. It's such a romantic view.'

He gestured further along the hills to the place where cars drove up and parked to enjoy the panoramic view of the landscape. 'Not quite as romantic as the kissing spot,' he joked.

Robin gazed up at him. 'Oh, I don't know. It's fairly romantic here.' Especially standing holding hands with Oliver. Wearing her flat pumps, he towered over her, and she felt shielded, protected.

He longed to kiss her, but held back, feeling it was too soon, and wanting to make their first moment special, not awkward.

Robin felt the same, and was happy just to stand there with him, looking at the vast sky, now a deep blue with stars twinkling all around them.

He sighed, wanting to stay longer, but knowing that she must be tired after driving all the way home after a busy day.

'Come on, I'll walk you down to your cottage.'

Smiling at him, she let him lead the way down the hill, steadying her when she almost toppled stepping over some of the heather.

She felt the strength in his arms as he grabbed hold of her. 'Steady there, we're halfway down.'

'These shoes aren't made for trudging the hills at night.'

Oliver agreed, so keeping the satchel slung on one shoulder, he lifted her up and carried her down the remainder of the hill.

Her laughter and squeals sounded in the night air as he carried her with ease.

'Shhh!' he scolded her jokingly. 'People will think I'm carrying you off into the night to have my wicked way with you.'

Robin laughed even more and tried not to think about how much this appealed to her. She was tired, extra tired, and excited about Oliver's news. This was her excuse and she was sticking with it. Though feeling herself wrapped in Oliver's strong arms did have a mischievous effect on her.

'I can hear your mind whirring, Robin, thinking bad thoughts.'

She laughed. 'Maybe, but I fully intend to behave myself.'

Oliver sighed and teased her. 'That's a pity.'

Her laughter filtered through the air and wafted into the night.

This was a time to remember, she told herself. Her first night of fun with Oliver.

But the night was far from over.

CHAPTER ELEVEN

Oliver put Robin gently down and smiled at her.

'Would you like me to help you carry your bags into your cottage?' he offered.

'Yes, thanks.'

While Oliver carried her bags, Robin dug out her keys, opened the front door and stepped inside. The cottage was in darkness and she turned the lights on in the hall and the living room.

Oliver followed her inside and put her bags down.

She wandered through to the kitchen. 'I'd offer you a cup of tea, but I've no milk.'

'Come and have a cup of tea with me. You'll be needing a cuppa after driving home.'

This made sense. Robin nodded. 'Just a quick cuppa.'

'Yes, come on,' he beckoned.

She left one of the lights on for when she came back home, turned the outside lantern on to give a glow to the front of the cottage, picked up her bag and followed Oliver outside.

He stood beside her car. 'We could walk there in a couple of minutes, or would you prefer to drive there?'

'I'd like to walk, get some fresh air. It's a lovely night.'

Happy with this decision, they walked side by side along the edge of the loch towards the main street. Again, she was aware that he towered over her.

She gazed at the loch and up at the stars. 'We're fortunate to live in such a lovely part of Scotland.'

Oliver completely agreed. 'It's the best move I've ever made.' Though having the nerve to ask Robin for a date was his crowning moment. He glanced at her walking along beside him, and for a second he sensed the couple they could be if they took their friendship to a loving relationship level. It felt great. He loved his art, but the one thing missing from his life was romance. Now there was a chance to make everything complete. But he wouldn't rush it, even though he longed to clasp her hand as they walked towards the main street.

Twinkle lights stretched between the lampposts, adding to the magical feel of the village. Night lights shone from several of the shop windows, including Fyn's flower shop, the sweet shop, quilt shop, Bradoch's bakery — and Oliver's art shop.

Oliver unlocked the door and flicked the lights on through the back in the kitchen.

He checked the fridge. 'Ah, the milk's upstairs in my kitchen.' His mind whirred, offering him two options. Run up and get the milk and bring it down to the shop, or invite Robin upstairs to his accommodation. If he chose the latter, would she think he was angling for a night of more than a friendly cuppa?

Robin smiled. 'Okay, lead the way.'

Trying not to look too delighted, he headed up the stairs and turned the lights on in his living room and the little kitchen just off it.

'Make yourself comfortable,' he said, running the water to fill the kettle.

Robin wandered around admiring the paintings on his living room walls. 'I love your artwork. These paintings are wonderful. Do you sell these too?'

'Some of them are for sale,' he called through to her. 'I hang them here as a sort of stock area. If I'm relaxing in the evenings, it gives me ideas for other pieces. But some I wouldn't part with.'

She heard the cups and spoons rattling as he prepared the tea.

'I'd find it difficult to part with any of these,' she called back to him.

He laughed. 'I'm a bit like that, but then I think of each painting hanging in someone else's house, being appreciated, and I like that.'

She stood in front of a large floral watercolour, so close she felt as if she was standing in its midst. The colours were vibrant, but with the transparent beauty that the watercolour created. Oliver's watercolour technique captured the feeling of being in a summer garden, lying in the sunshine, enjoying the fragrance and the beauty of the jasmine, roses, freesia, cornflowers and gerbera daisies.

'Are you hungry?' he called through.

'Peckish. A biscuit or two would be fine if you have them.'

He had a tin of luxury biscuits he'd bought from the wee shop. Only a couple of the chocolate wafers were missing. But then he had another idea.

'How about some hot buttered toast?'

'Oh, yes, if it's not too much bother. Toast would be great.' The thought of it gave her an appetite. She'd had afternoon tea at the modelling shoot, but then they'd been so busy taking the final photos she hadn't eaten dinner, preferring to jump in her car and head home before it was dark.

'I bought a loaf from Bradoch this morning.' He put four thick slices under the grill, set up plates and got the butter out of the fridge.

Robin continued to wander around, admiring the vibrant flower watercolours, and the oil landscapes and seascapes.

'Am I allowed to see your picture book art, or is it a secret until the book's published?' she said.

Oliver's laughter filtered through to the living room. 'I'll let you see the news on the publisher's website, and the other places the story has been highlighted. It's spread like wildfire.'

He flipped the toast, then ran through, turned on his laptop that was on the table in front of the sofa, and found the news on the publisher's website.

'Take a look at that while I keep an eye on the toast.' He hurried back through to the kitchen.

Robin sat on the comfy, floral chintz sofa and read the news. It included a sample page from the forthcoming picture book, a hint of the artwork, and a couple of great photos of Oliver. He looked so handsome. She felt her heart squeeze just looking at him.

She read the news piece and smiled. 'I love the characters, the cute wasps and bees, and butterflies, dragonflies and...' her words trailed off as she became engrossed in the editorial.

In the back of her mind she heard Oliver butter the toast, but she was lost in the colours of the artwork, the flowers in the summery cottage garden where the characters got up to all sorts of light–hearted adventures. There was enough information to convey what the book was about, without revealing too much of the details.

'What do you take in your tea?' he called through.

'Just milk, thanks.'

Scrolling through the website, she saw a video clip of Oliver demonstrating his artwork technique. It was only a couple of minutes long, but seeing him painting was wonderful.

Oliver carried a tray of tea and hot buttered toast through and put it down on the table beside the laptop.

'Help yourself.'

Robin lifted a slice of the toast and took a bite. 'Mmm,' she muttered.

Oliver sat down on the sofa beside her and lifted a slice.

Over tea and toast they talked about what they'd been up to, and about the forthcoming publicity in the newspaper the following day.

He showed her a copy of the pages for the picture book in a portfolio. 'These are copies of the artwork. I took the originals with me to London to give to the publisher. It's a thirty–two page book. Each page is a separate watercolour.'

'This is gorgeous. No wonder you've been offered a deal for more books in the series.' She looked through the portfolio at each page. 'So do you have to paint another thirty–two pieces of artwork for the next book?'

'I do.'

She sighed. 'You're going to be busy this summer.'

'With time off for fun.' He smiled at her.

Robin laughed. He had such a warm, sexy smile. She studied one of the characters in a pretty garden and as she gestured towards the bee, Oliver reached over to indicate that he'd included flowers from the loch. Their hands brushed against each other, and she felt a spark as they touched.

Oliver felt it too.

Robin blushed and he pretended not to notice as they continued to talk about the second book in the series.

'Do you know what the story will be for the next book?' she said.

'Yes, and I've discussed it with my agent and the publisher and they've agreed that they like it. That's what I was doing tonight, sketching ideas. It has a night setting, and I wanted to capture the feel of that.'

He reached over for his satchel and showed her what he'd sketched that evening.

'I won't tell anyone,' she assured him, appreciating that he trusted her with his work.

Oliver smiled. 'What do you think? They're obviously rough, but the night had such a wonderful glow to it.'

'The loch looks gorgeous. I love the atmosphere of these.'

'That's what I'm trying to capture. The atmosphere. The excitement of a summer evening.'

Robin was smiling at him, feeling herself falling a little bit more in love with Oliver.

'I can't promise that things won't get hectic from time to time,' he said. 'But I do promise that I'll make time for us to get to know each other. The way it would've been if I hadn't thought you were dating Gare.' He hesitated, wondering if he should tell her that she was part of the reason he'd finished the picture book.

She frowned, sensing a change in him. 'What is it?'

Come on, he urged himself. Tell her.

He took a deep breath. 'I was about to ask you out, to have dinner with me, months ago. I liked you the first time I saw you, and that has never changed. Anyway, when I heard that you were dating Gare, it hit me hard, so I dealt with my broken heartedness by working on the picture book in the evenings after I'd shut the shop for the day.'

Robin looked wide–eyed at him. 'I'd no idea.'

Oliver shrugged. 'I hid it well. No one knew until recently when I found out you weren't dating anyone. Then I had this overwhelming feeling that if I didn't step up and ask you out, some other man would step in.'

The realisation struck her. 'Jonathan.'

Oliver nodded firmly. 'Exactly.'

'Is that why you turned up at the cove when we were there?' She didn't mention about the effect he had on her when she saw him striding out of the sea in those trunks of his, all lean muscles and so sexy.

'Eh...yes,' he confessed. 'I talked myself into fighting for you. I didn't make a good job of it.'

'Oh, you did.' She blushed.

He laughed. 'You're blushing, Robin.'

'No wonder. Seeing you like that...wearing only those skinny dippers.'

He laughed again. 'We should have a day at the cove. You and me. We'll go swimming, have lunch, make a day of it.'

'Let's do that.'

Oliver made another round of tea, and then they sat together on the sofa talking about Oliver's picture book and Robin's textile art.

The night wore on without either of them watching the time, and somewhere along the line, snuggled up, they fell asleep and didn't wake until the morning.

A loud knock on the art shop's front door woke Oliver.

For a second, he forgot where he was. Not in his bed. He was on the sofa. Robin was sound asleep, snuggled into him.

'Robin,' he said urgently. 'Wake up. Someone's at the door.'

She blinked awake, an easy expression on her face, thinking she was in her bed at the cottage for a second, before the realisation struck her.

Another knock sounded from downstairs.

Robin jumped up, as did Oliver, and the two of them scrabbled around, trying to tidy themselves.

'Oliver!' Fyn shouted up to the window. 'I think you've slept in.'

He had. They had.

'I'll let Fyn in,' said Oliver.

'Okay, I'll hide. No. I'll scuttle out when he's not looking. Distract him.'

'How will I do that?'

'You'll think of something.'

Oliver ran down the stairs, finger brushing his hair, trying not to look like a man in a pickle.

Fyn stood outside the front door carrying a tray of little potted plants and a couple of packets of flower seeds.

Oliver opened the door, jammed it open so that Robin could make a clean escape, and welcomed Fyn in.

'I think I must've overslept,' said Oliver, forcing a tight smile. It wasn't a lie. He had. But he didn't mention he had Robin upstairs with him. They hadn't been up to anything, but the gossip would paint a different picture.

'These are summer seedlings I've been growing on the farm,' Fyn explained. 'It's a thanks for helping me put the blind up and loaning me the painting, which I'll remind you again, I'm buying.'

'Thanks. They look nice.' The flowers gave Oliver an instant excuse to guide Fyn through to the back of the shop and out into the garden.

The sun was already heating up the day, and dried the early morning dew.

Fyn took charge, setting the flowers up where he thought they'd gain the light but with enough shade so they could thrive.

'Water them once a day,' Fyn advised. 'Then when they're ready, I'll help you plant them in the garden.'

Oliver really did like the flowers. They reminded him of the flowers he'd pictured in his book.

'When I saw the news about your book and the wee creatures and the flowers you'd painted I thought you'd like these.'

'I do, it's ideal having them in my garden, to paint from real life, without having to head up to the loch or the fields,' Oliver told him.

'I'm pleased they'll be of use to you.' Fyn showed him the packets of seeds. 'These are my new summer garden mix. If you want to have a go at growing them, I'll bring you some containers and soil.'

'I'd love to have a go at growing my own flowers from seed.' Oliver was genuinely enthusiastic.

'Great. I'll bring some over later today. I'm sure you're going to be busy again.' He had a newspaper folded and tucked into the back pocket of his jeans. 'You're in the paper.' He handed it to Oliver.

'Near the middle. It's an interesting read and the photos of you are wonderful.'

Oliver scrabbled to find the page, and then stopped when he saw the photos. He hadn't expected that the one of him standing painting at the loch with Robin's cottage in the background would be so...large.

'They've given me a full feature!' Oliver exclaimed.

'You're infamous now,' Fyn said with a grin.

While they chatted, Robin crept down the stairs, trying to avoid the squeaky steps, and was about to make a stealthy run for it out the front door when Fyn came bounding through.

'I have to get back to my shop. I just popped over to give you the flowers,' Fyn said to Oliver.

Robin spun around, making it look like she'd just walked in, rather than bolting.

'Morning, Robin,' Fyn said, smiling. 'Your cottage is pictured in the paper.' He thumbed over his shoulder at Oliver.

Oliver was still reading the feature as he walked into the front shop.

Robin smiled guiltily. 'Morning, Fyn.' Then she looked at Oliver.

'Hello, Robin,' Oliver said, going along with the ruse. 'Fyn's brought the paper with the story in it.' He held the pages open and she came over for a look.

'Okay, I'll let you two lovebirds get on with it,' Fyn said, winking, knowing fine that Robin had stayed overnight.

Robin blushed as Fyn hurried away to his shop.

Oliver smiled at her. 'On a lighter note, the feature is excellent.'

'At least one piece of news today will be in our favour,' she said.

'I'll tell everyone you fell asleep. Nothing happened. I don't want your reputation being gossiped about.'

Robin gave him a look like that was never going to happen. The gossip would be rife, but maybe Oliver's news in the paper would make the main gossipmonger headlines.

CHAPTER TWELVE

The newspaper feature stole the community's interest that morning, but by the afternoon, the gossip about Oliver and Robin being romantically involved was being talked about. The whole scenario of the picture book deal, Oliver's trip to London, Robin's modelling, and Oliver skinny dipping in the sea caused a flurry of excitement and crossed wires.

Fyn had brought potting soil and containers to the art shop so Oliver could grow his own flowers from seeds.

They were outside in the shop's back garden.

Fyn showed him an easy method of planting the seeds in containers rather than directly into his garden.

Oliver was enjoying the process and taking a break in the sun away from the constant emails, messages and phone calls. He'd fielded numerous calls about his deal and the newspaper feature had stirred up a lot of interest in his paintings too. But he just needed a few minutes downtime and planting the seeds fitted the bill perfectly.

Oliver pressed the last of the seeds into one of the pots and sprinkled it with a liberal layer of rich soil.

'This is the soil I use,' said Fyn. 'You'll start to see wee sprouts shoot up if you sit the pots where they can get the sunlight but are sheltered from the cold and wind.'

'What about over there, near the hedge. It gets the midday sun and is sheltered,' Oliver suggested.

Fyn nodded, and then helped him move the pots over.

Oliver wiped the soil from his hands and stood for a moment admiring his achievement. 'I never thought it would be so easy or fun. I can see myself taking to gardening, so look out, I may start selling flowers in my shop,' he joked.

'Don't force me to get my crayons out,' Fyn countered. 'I haven't drawn anything since I was seven, but never say never.'

They laughed.

'While you're in a cheery mood,' Fyn began, 'you should know about the latest gossip.'

'About Robin and me?'

Fyn nodded.

Oliver knew about his romance with Robin being talked about, so he frowned, wondering what else they knew. Fyn hadn't told anyone about Robin's sleepover, so that snippet hadn't circulated.

'What's the latest gossip?' said Oliver.

'There's no way to sugar coat this one — folk think you went skinny dipping in the sea when you drove to the cove the day Robin was there with Jonathan.'

'Skinny dipping?'

'Yes, swimming without trunks. Enticing Robin with everything you had to outshine the sunshine.'

Oliver's smiled faltered. 'I was wearing trunks! Swimming trunks.'

Fyn shrugged. 'I did wonder, but...'

'That's the rumour?' Oliver's tone was incredulous.

'Yes. So steel yourself for the fun and the flack. Apparently, it's not just your paintings that are well hung.' Fyn could barely contain his mirth.

'What!' Oliver shouted. 'Who said that?'

'The source seems to be the crafting bee ladies.'

'Etta?' She was his first go–to for blame.

'No, it's Robin's fault for telling the ladies how buff you were walking out of the sea, dripping water, all manliness and muscles. Or words to that effect.'

'Robin is to blame for the gossip?' Oliver was flattered and flummoxed. Not in equal measures. Shame on him, but he was more flattered than anything else.

Fyn nodded and grinned. 'I think you really turned her head with your display at the cove.'

'There was nothing untoward on display,' Oliver protested, while still feeling flattered.

'I believe you. I didn't think you'd resort to that. You know what the gossip is like though, especially when Robin has been telling the ladies that you set her heart fluttering. And she didn't realise that you were...built.'

Oliver laughed nervously. 'The minx!' He gasped. 'She actually told the ladies that at the craft night?'

Fyn nodded. 'The women confide in each other, which they should, but it's just because of all the extra excitement about your books that's stirred up a whirlwind. It'll fade again, but I thought I should warn you if you get some smirking comments.'

'Thanks. I think.' Oliver shook his head. 'What about Robin? She'll be mortified.'

'No, Robin's in her cottage, sewing a new dress for the party, Aileen told me. The whole scenario and scandal hasn't hit her yet. Maybe it won't. By the time she emerges with a new frock, the gossip is like wildfire, and it'll be scorching something else by dinner time.'

Oliver tried not to smile.

Fyn joined him.

'I'm not sure what to do.'

'Hide, that would be my advice. Until it quietens down, hide in your shop, paint your new picture book, paint anything, and remember to water your flowers.'

Oliver nodded.

'Right, I'm away to get something to munch for afternoon tea from the bakery. Do you want anything?'

'Yes, ask Bradoch if he has one of his special cakes that combats embarrassment and being discombobulated,' Oliver joked.

Fyn laughed. 'Bradoch will have something for that, you can bet on it. I'll be back in a bit. Lock the front door. I'll approach back by stealth mode.'

Sharing the joke, Fyn ran across to the bakery.

Oliver swithered whether to lock the door or not.

Click. Decision made. Just to be on the safe side.

No sooner had he bolted himself into the shop, than his phone rang. It was his agent.

'I've just had call from a radio station,' his agent began. 'They want to invite you on to one of the shows next week to interview you. I hope you're up for it.'

'They want me to be on the radio?'

'Yes, it's one of the well–known stations, so great publicity. Come on, you should do it.'

'Okay, tell them I'll be there.'

'I'll phone them and find out the details, then call you back. How are you handling things in the village?'

Oliver told his agent the latest gossip.

He'd rarely heard his agent laugh so hard.

'I'm glad you're amused,' said Oliver, trying to sound miffed.

They finished the call with his agent's laughter still ringing happily.

Oliver took a deep breath, then he saw Fyn hurrying back with a white cake box.

Opening the door, Oliver let him in.

'I knew Bradoch would have something ideal.' Fyn put the box down on the counter and opened it. Four cakes were sitting inside, each one a different type and flavour.

'Bradoch gave me a selection for you. Apparently, these cover all events, so tuck in.'

'Two each,' said Oliver, eyeing the strawberry and cream whatever and the chocolate cake with chocolate sprinkles.

'You pick. They all look tasty to me.'

'Same here, but I'll have these two.' Oliver lifted them out and sat them on the counter.

Fyn was happy. 'I had my eye on the iced bun with fruit and cream, and the carrot cake.' He closed the lid and headed for the door.

'Cheers, Fyn,' Oliver called to him.

Fyn hurried away with the box, waving.

Oliver didn't lock the door this time.

He went through to the kitchen and put the kettle on for a cuppa. He'd have to face the gossip sometime. He might as well do it fired up on tea and cake.

'I didn't say that Oliver was skinny dipping!' Robin protested when Etta told her the news about the rumour. 'I said he was wearing his skinny dippers.'

'I know,' Etta assured her. She'd popped over to Robin's cottage to warn her about the gossip hotting up.

'Is that what people are talking about?' said Robin.

Etta nodded and folded her arms across her cardigan. 'Oliver is holed up in his shop. He sent out for emergency cakes from Bradoch's bakery.'

Robin blinked, and then started to see the funny side. 'Cakes?'

Etta explained. 'Aileen was in the bakery. She heard Fyn ask for cakes. He took them over to Oliver's shop. Oliver had locked himself in.'

'Can you circulate the gossip with the correct news that Oliver was wearing swimming trunks?'

'Yes, I'll do that. In fact, I've been doing that already, so no worries. I just wanted to let you know in case someone else told you.'

Robin smiled.

Etta gave her a reassuring hug. 'No one blames you for starting the gossip. We all know that Oliver is fit and sexy.'

Robin's smile faded. 'I didn't start the gossip.'

'Well, you sort of said how you were admiring Oliver's fit build, his lean muscles and all that.'

Robin paused. She had embellished a bit, but it was all true. She just didn't think her description of Oliver would become the latest gossip. 'Does Oliver know what I said?'

Etta stared, unblinking, wondering what to say.

'Right.' Robin sighed. 'He knows that I think he's gorgeous?'

'That's surely okay, isn't it?'

'Yes, fine,' Robin lied, inwardly wishing she'd kept her thoughts about him to herself.

'I'll away and let folk know that Oliver was wearing trunks,' said Etta.

Robin waved her off, then closed the door and wandered through to the kitchen. The back door was open letting in the warm, summery air. She could see the hills against the cobalt blue sky.

Fighting the urge to run for them, she made herself a cold glass of lemonade and pondered what to do when she had to face Oliver again.

Gaven had set a date for the party, a couple of nights from now, and she was planning to wear a white version of her blue chambray dress. It lay half finished beside her sewing machine in the living room. The white chambray would be pretty and light for the party dancing.

The only other party dress she had in her wardrobe that she hadn't worn to any of the events at the castle was a sparkly little cocktail dress that was tucked in the back, but had never been worn. She remembered buying it in a fashion boutique in the city. She hadn't needed or ever worn a sparkly cocktail dress, but the bargain and the rainy day had made her do something slightly wild. She'd gone into the boutique, tried the dress on, loved it and bought it. The dress had then hung in the back of her wardrobe. She'd always meant to wear it for a Christmas or New Year party, but it had yet to see the light of day, or rather, the glow of evening, even though she was sure it would outshine every other dress with its red sequins and shimmering silky red fabric.

Come on, she bolstered herself. She had to have something else in her wardrobe. She'd had a clear out of clothes she didn't wear when packing up to move to the cottage. The red dress made the cut, but there had to be another dress.

Rummaging through her wardrobe, she found a bag with a dress carefully folded inside it. She'd forgotten about this one. A floral print tea dress that was dressier than the white sundress she'd planned and less sparkly than the red. The fabric had heliotrope, lavender, thistles and flowers with a lilac theme. The colour suited her strawberry blonde hair.

Yes, this would be perfect. She hung it up on the outside of her wardrobe, and paired it with low heel comfy shoes for dancing.

She went through to her sewing machine and continued making the white chambray dress anyway. It would be handy for summery days.

But in the back of her mind she was still squirming with embarrassment about the latest gossip, but she felt confident that Etta would redress the balance of it. Wouldn't she?

Etta walked down to the main street and went into the art shop.

Oliver was in the back of the shop and came through hearing someone walk in.

The look on Etta's face suggested she wasn't there on business. She'd something on her mind and wanted to talk to him.

'What is it, Etta?'

'I've just been talking to Robin about the gossip. I want you to know that Robin didn't say you were skinny dipping. She said you were wearing skinny dippers, but somehow the story got mixed up and...well, you know the rumour.' She shrugged. 'It was just girl talk at the bee night. I'm letting folk know the correct version.'

'Thanks for letting me know. But can I ask...did Robin mention anything about me being...'

'Buff?'

Oliver gasped and laughed.

'If you're wondering if Robin admired you when you were swimming at the cove, she did. She may have over egged her description of you, and the ladies may have over exaggerated what she said. But yes, Robin likes you, if that's what you want to know.'

Oliver smiled and nodded. 'I thought I'd drop by her cottage when I close up the shop for the night, just to assure her.'

'You should. Hiding in your shop isn't a good look.'

'No, no, I won't be doing that.'

Etta smiled and changed the subject. 'I saw the feature in the newspaper. It was a corker. And

everyone is looking forward to the party at the castle.'
She then headed for the door.

'Thanks for stopping by, Etta,' he told her.

She smiled warmly and then walked away along
the street to Aileen's quilt shop to set the story right
with her.

The roast potatoes were sizzling nicely in the oven, but
on such a warm evening, Robin wished she'd cooked
something else for her dinner. But by the time
common sense had kicked in, the roast tatties were
half cooked, and the delicious aroma of them was
worth the heat.

She'd bought a bag of tatties and other groceries
from the wee shop after skulking out of Oliver's shop
earlier in the day, and had decided to make roasties for
her dinner.

As the tatties browned nicely to a light golden
crisp, she opened the kitchen door wide to let in the air
from the back garden, but the early evening had heated
up. The sun was burnishing everything in its golden
hour glow.

The tatties would be ready in less than ten minutes,
so she filled the kettle for tea and prepared a salad to
go with it. Most of the salad vegetables were fresh
from the local farms. The leafy lettuce was minty
fresh, and she sliced the tomatoes and added grated
carrot and greentails. A spoonful of coleslaw, local
tomato chutney and salad cream completed the
condiments.

With a couple of minutes to go, there was a knock
on the front door.

Wearing her grey leisure trousers and a short sleeve pink tee, she hurried through and peered out the living room window.

Oliver waved to her.

She went into the hall and called through to him. 'I'm not in.'

'I know that trick,' he countered.

'I'm hiding from sheer embarrassment.'

'That's a poor excuse.'

'I won't be cheery company.'

'I'll take my chances.'

Robin opened the door and looked suitable embarrassed, and yet their playful banter had taken the edge of the effects of the gossip.

'Something smells tasty,' he said, stepping inside.

'I'm making roast tatties.' She hurried down the hall to the kitchen. 'They'll be burnt roasties if I don't take them out of the oven.'

Oliver followed her and stood in the kitchen doorway, filling it as he had done before.

Robin was glad she could use the heat from the oven for the rosy blush on her cheeks.

'I don't want to interrupt your dinner. I'll come back later,' he offered.

'There's enough for two if you want to stay.'

He did.

'I'll rustle up more salad if you sort the tea.'

Oliver washed his hands at the sink, feeling at home with Robin.

Robin served up the roast potatoes and salad, and bread, while Oliver poured their tea.

They sat down at the kitchen table, keeping the door open to enjoy the evening air, while chatting about everything that had happened recently, and their plans for the following day and the party night at the castle.

'These roasties are delicious,' he said. 'I've barely stopped for anything to eat all day. Except Bradoch's cakes.'

She giggled. 'Emergency cakes.'

'Ah, so you heard.'

She nodded and smiled at him.

'What are you up to tomorrow?' he said.

'Pushing on with my textile art. I've had extra orders, so I plan to work on those. Etta's having a craft night at her cottage, so I'll pop along to that in the evening. I'm making another dress. A white version of the blue chambray one.'

'That'll be nice. It's handy that you can make a lot of your own clothes.'

'I'd like to do more dressmaking. Maybe I will. It depends on how busy I am this summer.'

'Someone could be taking up quite a bit of your time.' He smiled teasingly.

'I do hope so.'

'It's a promise.' He gazed over at her lovingly. 'I'll pick you up the following evening for the party.'

'I'll be ready. I'm looking forward to it.'

'So am I.'

Chatting and having their dinner, the evening went well, and when it was time for Oliver to leave, Robin stood at the front door to see him off.

He hesitated, and for a moment she thought he was going to kiss her goodnight, but he didn't, still wanting their first kiss to be extra special. Maybe at the party night, he'd thought, making it a night to remember.

Robin's day the next morning was busy, bright and bustling with activity. She'd had several extra orders for pieces of her textile art that were on sale on her website. She surmised that the publicity circulating around Oliver was highlighting businesses in the village.

Later, at the craft night at Etta's cottage, other members agreed that they'd seen an increase in their sales.

'I've had more orders of fabric and sales of my quilts from my shop,' Aileen told them as they chatted over tea, scones and shortbread.

'My knitted items have sold well,' Etta told them. 'But I wonder if it's through being involved with the knitwear company.' She shrugged. 'Either way, I've had a trip to the post office to send off a few orders today.'

'I love that blue yarn you're knitting with,' Sylvia said to Etta.

Etta held up the front of a cardigan she was knitting with the new yarn. 'Robin gave me it. It's from her modelling trip. The soft texture of the yarn is lovely to work with and it knits up well.'

The chatter included talk about what they were planning to wear to the party night.

Robin sat stitching the hem of her white dress. 'I was going to wear this, but then I found a floral print tea dress in my wardrobe, so I'm wearing that.'

'Remember to put on comfy shoes for dancing,' Etta reminded her.

'I will,' said Robin.

'Everyone's going to be there.' Aileen sounded excited.

Sylvia gave Aileen a nudge. 'Maybe Fyn will ask you to dance with him.'

Aileen tried not to blush. 'I'm sure we'll all be dancing with most of the men, including Bradoch and the laird.'

'I hope Gaven asks me to dance,' said Sylvia. 'I'm wearing a hot pink dress so maybe he'll notice me.'

'I'm wearing a summery blue dress I made months ago,' Aileen told them. 'It's got a drop waist and swishy skirt.'

'I plan to wear a ditsy print dress,' said Jessy. 'It's bound to be a warm night, and it's cotton and easy to dance in. Gaven's serving the vanilla ice cream with butterscotch at the buffet, along with other ice cream and trifle dishes. The hotel guests have been invited, and he says that they're all planning to attend, so it's going to be a lively night.'

'I think it's great that Gaven does this for the local community,' Robin told Jessy.

'Gaven's always been a great laird,' said Jessy. 'But although he wasn't looking for publicity, the castle bookings have increased. So everyone is getting the benefit of Oliver's achievement.'

'Bradoch is contributing a special cake for the party,' said Sylvia. 'He showed it to me this afternoon. It's a large chocolate cake and he's icing Oliver's name on it. He asked me for a selection of our chocolate button sweeties to decorate it. But keep this to yourselves.'

The ladies agreed to keep this secret, and then discussed their dresses for the party as the night wore on.

At the end of the evening, the members filtered out into the warm night, still chatting and buzzing with excitement.

Robin headed back to her cottage, enjoying the walk along the loch.

It was fairly late, so she decided to go to bed.

The moon shone in her bedroom window, and she saw dragonflies flitting through the evening air. Watching them and the light of the moon shimmering on the loch, she fell asleep.

Robin had showered, washed her hair and dried it smooth. It hung in silky waves around her shoulders. Her makeup emphasised her eyes and she wore a soft, deep rose lipstick.

The floral print dress flattered her figure, and she wore shoes that she could dance in.

Butterflies of excitement fluttered through her as Oliver knocked on the door to pick her up.

Grabbing her clutch bag, she turned the lights off, leaving the lantern lit, opened the front door and blinked when she saw Oliver standing there.

'You're wearing a kilt!'

'Yes, Gaven requested that kilts were worn, though I could've worn a suit if I wanted. But on a warm night like this, a kilt is fine for wearing for a party and dancing.'

Robin's heart reacted to seeing him looking so...sexy and handsome. With his dark tartan kilt he wore a cream lace–up ghillie shirt. Dark grey knee–length socks were worn with brogues.

'Is there something wrong with what I'm wearing?' he said.

'No,' she lied. Except that she hadn't thought he'd turn up wearing a kilt and lace–up shirt that exposed a tempting amount of his chest. He clearly hadn't done this deliberately to set her senses alight, but she couldn't help wonder if Oliver was the traditional type and had gone commando under his kilt.

Oliver gestured to his car. 'Shall we?'

Hiding the effect he had on her behind a smile, she let him seat her in the car and drive off towards the castle. The drive was only minutes, and she realised she'd never been driven anywhere by a kiltie. Unknown to Oliver, he was driving her a little bit wild with how handsome he looked.

'You look beautiful,' Oliver told her as they drove the short distance to the castle. Within minutes, they were heading through the front entrance towards the car park. It was busy with cars, but he found somewhere to park and escorted her into the castle.

Music and chatter sounded from the reception, and the chandeliers gave a welcoming glow as they walked in.

Gaven was at the reception talking to Jessy, and he smiled and came to welcome them.

'Good evening,' said Gaven. He wore his kilt and a highland dress shirt and tie. He looked very smart. He gestured towards the function room where the buffet was set up along one wall. Couples were already taking to the dance floor, and the atmosphere pulled them into the heart of the party.

Etta and several of the crafting bee ladies were standing chatting. Some had their husbands or boyfriends with them, but they all smiled when they saw Oliver and Robin.

A local live band played on a small stage area, and Gaven stepped up to make an announcement, welcoming Oliver and congratulating him on his picture book achievement.

'I'm happy that Oliver came for a holiday here and liked it so much he decided to stay in our little community. I'm sure we all want to wish Oliver success with his new books.'

Everyone clapped and cheered, raised their glasses in a toast, and the evening was officially started.

Oliver tipped his glass of whisky against Robin's glass. 'Here's to us, Robin. You and me.'

'Cheers, Oliver.'

Etta beckoned them over and they joined the group of bee members. Etta wore a navy blue dress that really suited her, and all the ladies were wearing their party dresses, while the men wore kilts.

'You're both looking great,' Etta told them.

'And you're looking lovely this evening, Etta,' said Oliver.

'Come and cut your cake,' Bradoch said, tugging Oliver's arm and including Robin.

Gaven was there to take a photograph of the chocolate cake, iced with Oliver's name.

Bradoch lit the candles on the cake. 'Make another wish, Oliver.'

Taking a deep breath, Oliver blew the candles out in one go, and made another wish involving a happy ever after with Robin. Then he cut the cake.

Oliver was quite overcome with the kindness and genuine warmth from everyone, and the effort from individuals, like Bradoch, for making a special cake.

Amid the revelry, the first reel of the night was announced.

Oliver clasped Robin's hand. 'Are you ready?'

'No,' she said, smiling up at him.

Oliver laughed.

Fyn took hold of Aileen's hand and led her into the circle. He clasped hold of Robin's hand too, so she found herself between Fyn and Oliver.

Bradoch joined in, holding Aileen's other hand, and she beamed with glee at Etta as she was sandwiched between two handsome kilties.

Gare hurried over to Sylvia before anyone else claimed the dance.

'Will you dance with me, Sylvia?' said Gare, offering her his hand.

Sylvia was happy to dance with the tall, blond farmer, and even more excited as Gaven clasped her other hand as the music kicked in and the reel began.

It was fast–moving and fun, and Robin found herself being whirled around the dance floor, feeling the energy of the dance and those involved.

The chocolate cake and the buffet were delicious, and between the dancing, and chatting to people about his news, Oliver rarely let go of Robin's hand. They were clearly a couple enjoying their first official night together.

As the night wore on, and a slow dance wound the evening to a happy close, Oliver held Robin in his arms as they waltzed around the floor.

For the finale, Gaven had arranged something they often had for engagement or birthday parties.

At midnight, a flurry of balloons was released from the ceiling on to the dance floor.

Robin glanced up, seeing the balloons cascade down all around them, feeling in that moment that she was where she was supposed to be, with the man she was supposed to be with — Oliver.

Oliver pulled her close. 'Would it be okay now if I kissed you?'

Robin nodded and smiled. 'I think so,' she said softly, gazing lovingly at Oliver.

She'd fallen in love with him.

He'd long been in love with her.

Leaning down, Oliver kissed her again and again, making the moment last.

A cheer rose up around them, and blinking out of their romantic bubble, Oliver and Robin smiled at all their friends.

'I love you, Robin,' Oliver whispered to her, and kissed her again.

'I love you too, Oliver.'

At the end of the evening as he drove her home to her cottage, he asked her out on a special date.

'Would you like to go swimming with me tomorrow at the cove?' said Oliver. 'Not skinny dipping.'

Robin laughed. 'I'd love to.'

He pulled up outside her cottage, leaned over and kissed her. 'I'll pick you up after breakfast. We'll make a day of it. Have lunch. Swim in the afternoon.'

'It sounds great,' Robin said, feeling that this was the start of many wonderful times together, a happy and exciting life with Oliver and a future together by the loch.

End

About the Author:

De-ann Black is a bestselling author, scriptwriter and former newspaper journalist. She has over 100 books published. Romance, thrillers, espionage novels, action adventure. And children's books (non-fiction rocket science books and children's fiction). She became an Amazon All-Star author in 2014 and 2015.

She previously worked as a full-time newspaper journalist for several years. She had her own weekly columns in the press. This included being a motoring correspondent where she got to test drive cars every week for the press for three years.

Before being asked to work for the press, De-ann worked in magazine editorial writing everything from fashion features to social news. She was the marketing editor of a glossy magazine.

She is also a professional artist and illustrator. Embroidery design, fabric design, dressmaking, sewing, knitting and fashion are part of her work.

Additionally, De-ann has always been interested in fitness, and was a fitness and bodybuilding champion, 100 metre runner and mountaineer. As a former N.A.B.B.A. Miss Scotland, she had a weekly fitness show on the radio that ran for over three years.

De-ann trained in Shukokai karate, boxing, kickboxing, Dayan Qigong and Jiu Jitsu. She is currently based in Scotland.

Her 16 colouring books are available in paperback, including her latest Summer Nature Colouring Book and Flower Nature Colouring Book.

Her latest embroidery pattern books include: Floral Garden Embroidery Patterns, Christmas & Winter Embroidery Patterns, Floral Spring Embroidery Patterns and Sea Theme Embroidery Patterns.

Website: Find out more at: www.de-annblack.com

Fabric, Wallpaper & Home Decor Collections:
De-ann's fabric designs and wallpaper collections, and home decor items, including her popular Scottish Garden Thistles patterns, are available from Spoonflower.
www.de-annblack.com/spoonflower

Also by De-ann Black (Romance, Action/Thrillers & Children's books). See her Amazon Author page or website for further details about her books, screenplays, illustrations, art, fabric designs and embroidery patterns.

Amazon Author page:
www.De-annBlack.com/Amazon

Romance books:

Snow Bells Haven series:
1. Snow Bells Christmas
2. Snow Bells Wedding
3. Love & Lyrics

Scottish Highlands & Island Romance series:
1. Scottish Island Knitting Bee
2. Scottish Island Fairytale Castle
3. Vintage Dress Shop on the Island
4. Fairytale Christmas on the Island

Scottish Loch Romance series:
1. Sewing & Mending Cottage
2. Scottish Loch Summer Romance
3. Sweet Music

Quilting Bee & Tea Shop series:
1. The Quilting Bee
2. The Tea Shop by the Sea
3. Embroidery Cottage
4. Knitting Shop by the Sea
5. Christmas Weddings

Sewing, Crafts & Quilting series:
1. The Sewing Bee
2. The Sewing Shop
3. Knitting Cottage (Scottish Highland romance)
4. Scottish Highlands Christmas Wedding

The Cure for Love Romance series:
1. The Cure for Love
2. The Cure for Love at Christmas

Cottages, Cakes & Crafts series:
1. The Flower Hunter's Cottage
2. The Sewing Bee by the Sea
3. The Beemaster's Cottage
4. The Chocolatier's Cottage
5. The Bookshop by the Seaside
6. The Dressmaker's Cottage

Scottish Chateau, Colouring & Crafts series:
1. Christmas Cake Chateau
2. Colouring Book Cottage

Summer Sewing Bee

Sewing, Knitting & Baking series:
1. The Tea Shop
2. The Sewing Bee & Afternoon Tea
3. The Christmas Knitting Bee
4. Champagne Chic Lemonade Money
5. The Vintage Sewing & Knitting Bee

Tea Dress Shop series:
1. The Tea Dress Shop At Christmas
2. The Fairytale Tea Dress Shop In Edinburgh
3. The Vintage Tea Dress Shop In Summer

The Tea Shop & Tearoom series:
1. The Christmas Tea Shop & Bakery
2. The Christmas Chocolatier
3. The Chocolate Cake Shop in New York at Christmas
4. The Bakery by the Seaside
5. Shed in the City

Christmas Romance series:
1. Christmas Romance in Paris
2. Christmas Romance in Scotland

Oops! I'm the Paparazzi series:
1. Oops! I'm the Paparazzi
2. Oops! I'm Up To Mischief
3. Oops! I'm the Paparazzi, Again

The Bitch-Proof Suit series:
1. The Bitch-Proof Suit
2. The Bitch-Proof Romance
3. The Bitch-Proof Bride
4. The Bitch-Proof Wedding

Heather Park: Regency Romance
Dublin Girl
Why Are All The Good Guys Total Monsters?
I'm Holding Out For A Vampire Boyfriend

Action/Thriller books:

Knight in Miami
Agency Agenda
Love Him Forever
Someone Worse

Electric Shadows
The Strife Of Riley
Shadows Of Murder
Cast a Dark Shadow

Children's books:

Faeriefied
Secondhand Spooks
Poison-Wynd

Wormhole Wynd
Science Fashion
School For Aliens

Colouring books:

Summer Nature
Flower Nature
Summer Garden
Spring Garden
Autumn Garden
Sea Dream
Festive Christmas
Christmas Garden
Christmas Theme

Flower Bee
Wild Garden
Faerie Garden Spring
Flower Hunter
Stargazer Space
Bee Garden
Scottish Garden
Seasons

Embroidery Design books:

Sea Theme Embroidery Patterns
Floral Garden Embroidery Patterns
Christmas & Winter Embroidery Patterns
Floral Spring Embroidery Patterns
Floral Nature Embroidery Designs
Scottish Garden Embroidery Designs

Printed in Great Britain
by Amazon